TO PIE

Henry Parland

HENRY PARLAND was born in Vyborg, Karelia, in 1908, the eldest son of a Russian government engineer, with German and (distant) English origins, and a mother of German and Baltic descent. Until Henry was four, the family lived in St Petersburg and Kiev, but then settled in the Vyborg area (Finland was part of the Russian Empire from 1809 until 1917). The revolutionary years were hard, assets were lost and Oswald Parland did not manage to get home until 1920. The family then moved to the outskirts of Helsinki in 1921, settling in Grankulla. Henry grew up speaking German and Russian. His initial schooling had been in German, but at the age of 14 he switched to a Swedish-speaking school and began to write in Swedish. Under paternal pressure he enrolled to study law at Helsinki University in 1927, but was mainly committed to his writing and made an early breakthrough into modernist circles; the avant-garde magazine *Quosego* published some of his early poems and prose. Henry's studies stagnated as he enjoyed the buzzing life of 1920s Helsinki. His father Oswald eventually despaired and, in 1929, dispatched his son to Kaunas (then the capital of Lithuania) to be near his philosopher uncle, Vilhelm Sesemann. Henry worked at the Swedish consulate and wrote for various Finland-Swedish and Lithuanian periodicals. He also began a novel: *Sönder, To Pieces,* which was partly inspired by his reading of Proust, but also bears witness to a fascination with film, jazz and the modernist movement in Russia and elsewhere. He had completed the main manuscript by late summer 1930 and was still reworking it when, on 10 November, he died of scarlet fever. Since 1932, several editions of *Sönder* have been published, culminating in Per Stam's critical edition of 2005.

DINAH CANNELL recently retired as a freelance interpreter. Her translation of *To Pieces* came slowly together over a number of busy years. She now lives in Bristol.

Some other books from Norvik Press

Kjell Askildsen: *A Sudden Liberating Thought* (translated by Sverre Lyngstad)

Victoria Benedictsson: *Money* (translated by Sarah Death)

Hjalmar Bergman: *Memoirs of a Dead Man* (translated by Neil Smith)

Jens Bjørneboe: *Moment of Freedom* (translated by Esther Greenleaf Mürer)

Jens Bjørneboe: *Powderhouse* (translated by Esther Greenleaf Mürer)

Jens Bjørneboe: *The Silence* (translated by Esther Greenleaf Mürer)

Johan Borgen: *The Scapegoat* (translated by Elizabeth Rokkan)

Kerstin Ekman: *Witches' Rings* (translated by Linda Schenck)

Kerstin Ekman: *The Spring* (translated by Linda Schenck)

Kerstin Ekman: *The Angel House* (translated by Sarah Death)

Kerstin Ekman: *City of Light* (translated by Linda Schenck)

Arne Garborg: *Tha Making of Daniel Braut* (translated by Marie Wells)

P. C. Jersild: *A Living Soul* (translated by Rika Lesser)

Selma Lagerlöf: *Lord Arne's Silver* (translated by Sarah Death) (2011)

Selma Lagerlöf: *The Löwensköld Ring* (translated by Linda Schenck) (2011)

Selma Lagerlöf: *The Phantom Carriage* (translated by Peter Graves) (2011)

Viivi Luik: *The Beauty of History* (translated by Hildi Hawkins)

Henri Parland: *To Pieces* (translated by Dinah Cannell) (2011)

Amalie Skram: *Lucie* (translated by Katherine Hanson and Judith Messick)

Amalie and Erik Skram: *Caught in the Enchanter's Net: Selected Letters* (edited and translated by Janet Garton)

August Strindberg: *Tschandala* (translated by Peter Graves)

August Strindberg: *The Red Room* (translated by Peter Graves)

Hanne Marie Svendsen: *Under the Sun* (translated by Marina Allemano)

Hjalmar Söderberg: *Martin Birck's Youth* (translated by Tom Ellett)

Hjalmar Söderberg: *Selected Stories* (translated by Carl Lofmark)

Anton Tammsaare: *The Misadventures of the New Satan* (translated by Olga Shartze and Christopher Moseley)

Ellen Wägner: *Penwoman* (translated by Sarah Death)

TO PIECES

(on the developing of Velox paper)

by

Henry Parland

Translated
by
Dinah Cannell

With an Afterword
by
Per Stam

Norvik Press
2011

First published as: *Sönder (om framkallning av Veloxpapper)*.
Published by Svenska litteratur sällskapet i Finland, Helsinki
Atlantis, Stockholm, 2005

A catalogue record for this book is available from the British Library.

ISBN: 9781870041874

Norvik Press
Department of Scandinavian Studies
University College London
Gower Street
London WC1E 6BT
United Kingdom

Website: www.norvikpress.com
E-mail address: norvik.press@ucl.ac.uk

Managing editors: Sarah Death, Helena Forsås-Scott, Janet Garton, C.
Claire Thomson.

Cover illustration: Based on a detail of Albert Edefelt's painting
Nyländska Jaktklubben Harbour in Helsinki (1899), © Finnish National
Gallery. Source: Central Art Archives. Photographer: Hannu Karjalainen.

Layout: Elettra Carbone
Cover design: Essi Viitanen and Elettra Carbone

Printed in the UK by Lightning Source UK Ltd.

Contents

Translator's Foreword..6

To Pieces
I - The writer inspects himself in the mirror............................9
II - On taking photographs and developing prints.................13
III - Ami is coming...16
IV - Ami is sad...20
V - On hats..24
VI 31
VII 34
VIII 39
IX - I take fright...44
X 48
XI 51
XII 61
XIII 68
XIV 75
XV 77
XVI 79
XVII 84
XVIII 93
XIX 97
Epilogue - 100

Afterword by Per Stam...103
Literature..116

Translator's Foreword

In what follows I have tried to convey to the English-speaking reader some of the wonderment I felt when first coming across this short novel by Henry Parland.

It is composed in a Swedish that is very much the writer's own: fresh, vibrant, pithy – and syntactically a little surprising.

Parland's odd linguistic background may explain some of this, as Per Stam's Afterword lays out. Per's flowing, yet scholarly appraisal offers an account of the work's genesis and place within the literary world of the 1930.

Translation studies speaks of foreignizing and domestication, of readability and colonial appropriation. My goal has been to produce a text that is – I hope – pleasant to read, yet retains its special, dissonant and foreign edge.

Dinah Cannell
Bristol November 2010

Motto: This book is perhaps a plagiarism of Marcel Proust

I

The writer inspects himself in the mirror

Before he began writing this novel the writer took his mirror from the washstand, placed it in front of him and inspected his face. It was somewhat elongated, neither out of the ordinary nor without its personal stamp. The eyes were grey and weary, the hair dark, struggling back from the forehead to settle, smooth and thick, above the ears. The mouth was a bit bored and heavy, eager to convey irony – but that required effort. And effort cut two extended streaks at either corner. The chin kept its counsel.

Overall the impression was of tentativeness, coupled with a strong sense of self. Sometimes one trait predominated, sometimes the other, depending on his humour, which in turn was dictated by the interplay and harmony between his tie and the invariably semi-starched and long-tipped collar. All this duly correlated with a host of external factors such as a ready supply of money, cigarettes, sensory input, etc. The writer was nonetheless in rotten humour on occasions, flawless collar tips notwithstanding. But further probing on this front would take us farther than we might wish to go, so suffice it to say: he was a man of moods.

The mirror reflected his image disinterestedly. It had done so several times a day for one and a half years and was now thoroughly sick of the writer's physiognomy and ties. Mirrors (leaving aside the more phlegmatic pocket variety) are like camera lenses in that they tire incredibly fast of forever seeing the same old face. So that a shaving mirror veritably craves the occasional sight of a pouting female mouth working in its lipstick. And a Zeiss-Ikon lens becomes blurred and out of focus when called upon to photograph the same person several times over. The writer's mirror was no exception. It reflected his jaded

9

and yawning face and, when he continued to stare regardless, grimaced.

Knife-like, the streaks at the mouth's corners clove his features, eye symmetry was lost and the chin gaped contemptuously down. The writer stuck out his tongue at his mirror image, which immediately did likewise; then he lit a cigarette and started to write. He began with a love letter.

You died a year ago last week, Ami, and I owe you an apology for failing to mark the occasion until now. Goodness knows why I so completely and utterly forgot; I can't even remember what I was doing on the day. Probably sitting in the consulate, flicking through stiff, impersonal papers and looking out of the window. It was raining. Although I actually can't remember too clearly. – Maybe I'm getting mixed up with this time last year. Then it rained all autumn: fine, sharp drops that seeped through clothes, stinging one to a shiver. As we walked home from your funeral, all Sten and I wanted to do was slip in somewhere for a reviving cup of hot coffee. We made for Hotel Kämp on the Esplanade. The café there was so empty that we were in two minds about going in. We sat for two hours talking business.

Rolf approached as we were about to leave. Sten told him we'd been to your funeral. Rolf's spectacles flashed uncomprehendingly. Then something seemed to spring into his mind. "Indeed, indeed," he said and proceeded on his way, holding himself a bit too stiffly.

But the last thing I want to do is gossip about your old friends, Ami. Rolf was uncharacteristically vague that day and I'm sure he thought better of his behaviour afterwards. Not to mention the fact that we were standing in the hotel lobby, with people running up and down stairs and doors banging and confusing everyone. He can't have known whether he was coming or going.

I'm sure therefore you'll forgive Rolf and me for failing, each in our own way, to fret enough over your death. My trouble is that I forget things so incredibly fast. Almost faster than you – and you weren't half good at it. Writing to you as I am now – and there's a matter I wish to raise with you, almost a business proposition – it is not easy to hit a direct, personal note. I do not see you clearly enough anymore. Well, I can maybe just about force my brain to focus in on your every detail, but the image simply doesn't come to life. Six months back it was another story. But what a difference six months can make!

Do you realize you've been elevated to the status of some kind of saint? When speaking of you these days it has become obligatory to adopt a dolefully official tone of voice. (Sickening as it admittedly is, I am probably partly to blame.) All these people seem to have forgotten that you were a human being; in their eyes you are but an accretion of fine traits and qualities. I'm sure you don't much care for that – pretty sure, anyway. Which brings me on to the matter I wish to raise with you – almost a proposal, as I mentioned earlier – and I do hope you'll oblige. Don't worry, it's nothing terrible! I even have an inkling you might like the idea, although I'm having some trouble expressing myself. Hence this long introduction.

Look, Ami, I'd like to write this book about you. With your permission of course. I want to write you down as I remember you and I'd very much appreciate your assistance. The manner of that assistance doesn't matter too much. You'll doubtless have your limitations: you are dead, after all. Yet you could still potentially help me find a way of not leaving anything out; of getting you properly defined and alive before my eyes. Your cooperation would be much appreciated.

Look, I want to have you in front of me again as you were, not as the badly painted icon people have since turned you into. I must smash that icon to pieces, for it is not you. Your job is to assist.

I intend to tear your image from every nook of my soul and write it down on narrow-lined, white vellum paper. Maybe it will hurt. There is undeniably a touch of brutality involved. Yet the key, I'm sure, is to prise you free from all the preconceived notions you're tangled up with, which stop me from seeing you there in front of me.

You're afraid you'll end up dying on me all over again? Darling Ami, in that case just think of those moments of life before you fade out and this book reaches completion. If you are prepared to help me with the writing, that is. And what happens next? Goodness me, we've only just begun – and here you are worrying about the end!

Anyway, even if you're not up for it, I've at least done the decent thing and notified you of my decision. It's a pity I had to disturb you in that case, but the damage is now done. I'll wish you goodnight then, Ami. Think it over. We ought ideally to start tomorrow evening. I'll be waiting for you around 10. Any earlier probably wouldn't be a good idea; there's too much light during the daytime. So, I'll see you at 10 tomorrow evening. Sleep well.

Henry

II
On taking photographs and developing prints.

I am the owner of a Zeiss-Ikon camera: 6 x 9 cm plates; aperture: F/6.3. My preferred choice was the F/4.5 model, but it would have cost nearly twice as much and my finances could not stretch to that in one go. The camera has been with me now for three years and I've spent a fortune on plates, accessories and developing.

Once upon a time I took pictures of landscapes, but now only do individual and group portraits. Landscape photographs are constantly trying to pass themselves off as high art – neither proper nor feasible in my opinion. A photograph should settle for capturing every last detail of a situation and nothing more. Therefore it will always be the snapshot of a moment. Exposure times longer than 1/5th of a second run counter to the very essence of photography.

I always do my own developing. Three or four times a year I am gripped by a furious urge to develop and print plates taken several months earlier and left lying for so long in the cupboard, wrapped in their light-resistant paper, that I cannot even remember what they depict. I lock myself into my room, screw a red bulb into the lamp and mercilessly sweep everything off the desk. On it I place baths containing water, developer and acid fixing salts, purchased that same day and dissolved by an ecstatic me in a measuring jug full of hot water.

Metol-hydroquinone is my favourite developer. It is handy to use and, given my tendency to get carried away when working on negatives, the likelihood of mistakes being made in the heat of the moment is reduced. I am also partial to Agfa's double-sided glass capsules, with their soft tinfoil casing which tears open more readily than a living body, allowing the powder to stream out in white, vitreous grains. Fixing salts, on the other hand, fill me with a certain hostility. Their crystals behave in far too demanding and self-assured a fashion as they plop noisily to the bottom of the glass.

I lay the plate in the bath and let the developer glide caressingly over the gelatine membrane, which blushes slightly at the touch of the red lamplight on its pale, matt hue. I sway the bath back and forth and my heart beats ever faster. And when, like a burgeoning flush, the first dark flecks on the plate begin to emerge, the experience reaches its climax. Henceforward I perform with a perfectly cool head as I make the necessary adjustments to shade and intensity. Further mistakes are rare; my hands work with machine-like precision and I experience a weary limpness inside – until the plate in question is sufficiently darkened and the next can be plunged into the bath. Then I surge back to life.

Semi-matt, soft paper is my favourite when it comes to printing negatives, for it offers greater depth and does not distort the image in the way that hard or glossy paper can sometimes do. And whereas developing negatives is a rather theoretical activity – you can only guess at the final result from the density and sharpness of the black swathes – printing renders the miracle real. All at once a face, a landscape, stares out from the pure white sheet, just as you remember, yet clouded by impressions and associations too indistinct to be properly removed. Here in the bath, rosily tinged by the red light from the bulb, that blurred and clouded impression reclines intact, sharply differentiated from everything around it, and detailed in a way that only a camera lens – never a human eye – can capture.

The whole joy of a photograph lies in those previously unobserved details; once you are accustomed to them and your image of the subject in question is complete, the picture itself is of no further interest. A photograph thus turns out to have a very short lifespan. After just a few hours it appears rather forlorn and bygone and is best put aside and forgotten – until one day, by chance, you are visited by that same sense of immediacy and novelty that comes when small and trivial details make the remembrance of something quite removed and forgotten flash up with all the compelling brightness and suggestive illusion of reality. Never do you get a stronger sense of this than when you are bent over a developing bath and feature after feature bursts forth, each one complementing – giving new meaning and weight to – the next and finally coalescing as a picture which, wide-eyed, takes in the room like a newborn child.

A prime instance is when you are printing negatives of faces and groups. There is something of an awakening from the dead in the process. A state of affairs or an expression which in real life is never repeated can now be reproduced at will, the only requirement being an adequate supply of printing paper and developer. You can create hundreds of copies of the features of a person who died many years ago. You can fill your whole room with pictures, one identical to the next and all smiling or staring in the same manner. Pretty much a guaranteed way to go mad if photographs did not have such a short lifespan that they managed, after just a few hours, to forsake their lifelike selves and transmogrify into forlorn and superficial reproductions of something not even worth a second thought.

III
Ami is coming.

– It's five to ten. Ami should be here in five minutes. Everything is ready for her. I have placed on the table two bowls, one for developer and one for fixing salts; also a printing frame, two packets of Velox paper and a pile of carefully stacked negatives.
– And there's a red bulb brooding on the ceiling.

I myself am decked out in wondrous ceremonial attire. She'll most likely laugh her semi-amused, semi-vacant laugh when she catches sight of my apocryphal, stained trousers; not to mention the jacket, which is now too tight across the chest and has therefore popped a button. In a tone of half-hearted reproach she will say: could you not sew on a new one? And, out of habit, she will scornfully raise a pencilled eyebrow.

I pick up the printing frame, drop in a negative and cover it protectively with the sheet of paper, which presses somewhat reluctantly against the gelatine membrane, softly arching like the back of a cat as it stretches awake. I put on the lid and stare, overwhelmed, into the lamplight. It flares up for 40 seconds and my terrified and trembling eyes – caught in the flood of light spilling into the room and battling energetically with the infernal light from the bulb on the ceiling – come to a halt with a desperate spasm as they settle on the clock – 10 seconds, 20 seconds 25, 35, 37, 39,

– 40 seconds.

The white light fades out as fast as it flared up; the bulb shines redder still with the glow of victory. I press the paper into the developing bowl and my breath grows fiery and alert.

Ami is coming.

She comes tentatively, holding back, and the developer presses her features out from the paper in the form of dark blobs, which soon fall into line, grow darker and converge in an intimation of Ami's tired, fair head. I nervously shake the tray and the liquid rocks back and forth, giving life and expression to her face. It lights up, the features grow more and more familiar – and now she smiles. She always smiled when I took her picture. A smile suited her and she knew it.

Good day Ami, I say softly. She curls her lips a little, for my hands have been shaking and a shiver runs across the surface of the developer.

How are things, Ami? I ask. It was good of you to come. By the way, how about the little matter I spoke of yesterday – – You won't help – –?

Ami's face has darkened somewhat. Then the surface of the developer shivers afresh as I blow the words in its direction and she nods with a smile. – I'm not quite sure as yet, but we could try. And anyway, you'd better take me out of the bowl unless you want to destroy my complexion for good. Look how sunburnt I've got already. You'd think I'd spent my whole life on the beach. Hurry up!

I come to my senses with a jolt and pull the picture out of the bowl.

The smile on Ami's lips has stiffened into a horizontal slash and her face is shaded by a dark veil. The print is ruined.

– –My darling Ami, I'm so sorry for this clumsy welcome, but when I saw your sweet little face I could remember neither how to behave nor how to develop Velox paper. Are you angry with me, Ami? Please don't be. You looked so friendly just now, so do give it another go. I was simply really glad to see you, that's all. – You feel I've ruined your lovely complexion? Unforgiveable of me, I admit. But between us we can fix the damage, you know. We'll do a fresh picture of you. Provided you don't smile again and make me lose my head. Try to keep a serious face until I've put you in the fixing salt solution!

Ami's image stares reproachfully past me. It looks old and indifferent – like she sometimes does in the morning after a late night. I sling the negative into the water bath and it lands upside down. – You seem a bit annoyed, Ami. Don't you think me capable of giving you a proper welcome?

I place a new piece of paper in the copying frame. I work in cold and calculating fashion, but my heart thumps with apprehension. When Ami's face begins to shape itself into a smile in the bowl, I turn away and count to ten. Yes!

Bright and happy, she looks out from the bowl of fixing salts. Her smile is a bit surprised and she blinks somewhat bemusedly at the sudden release of white light from the table lamp. But she soon gets used to it and – once I have placed her in the water bath – she begins to speak; hesitantly at first and then more and more fluently, like someone who has been alone for a long time and therefore feels uneasy at suddenly finding herself among people again.

On her forehead, just below the hairline, I can see a small, dark speck where the negative must have got damaged, although I never noticed before. It gives her face a completely new expression, more serious somehow than the one I associate with the Ami I used to know. I say:

– Did you bump your head on the way over, Ami? I'm so sorry that your visit here has been such a trial. First I went and messed up your lovely complexion; then you were so good as to come again regardless and you've ended up with a bang on the head. Does it still hurt? The water in the bowl ought to be good for dabbing your forehead. What do you think?

Ami smiles. The table lamp casts saucy little reflexions across the picture, which looks at me in a friendly way.

– Oh, don't worry. I hadn't really expected any better a welcome. I know you well enough, for heaven's sake. Do you remember when you were trying to be polite and nearly twisted my ankle because you insisted on helping me with my galoshes? And I couldn't care less about that bump. The water may well be lukewarm now, but then you specially ran me a hot bath, remember?

– We both laugh. The water ripples with a tight succession of little waves which echo Ami's muffled, gay laugh. But she suddenly turns serious and looks about her in the room.

– Everything's the same as before, I see. Yet it's over a year since I was last here. But you certainly look a lot more dishevelled than you did. What on earth have you got on? You should be ashamed of yourself, giving me a welcome like this. You look like – –

– I'm so sorry, Ami, I say. It's not that I'm more dishevelled than when I last saw you. But I have become more sensible. That magic potion I availed myself of to awaken you from the dead leaves truly dreadful marks on one's clothing. Hence this ceremonial attire.

She scrutinizes me. You said something about a business deal in your letter. But you don't look too creditworthy to me.

– That was a turn of phrase, Ami. And you need have no hesitation about granting me credit now. I have a permanent position.

Okay, okay. We'll see about that. But I don't really know what you plan to do with me. Perhaps have me nude. Or dress me in pyjamas? I think I'd prefer the latter.

– You'll have blue-striped, silken pyjamas. I promise. And not just one pair, but loads.

– The picture sinks slowly to the bottom of the bowl. I'll think about it. But get me out of here right now. I'm freezing.

IV
Ami is sad.

On the table there are pieces of paper which have curled up with a shiver and developed coarse rough goose flesh. I unroll them and endeavour to smooth out their anxious bodies. They resist and, when I resort to violence to flatten them, they make little rustling noises.

– Stop being so rough, Ami says, it hurts. You're twisting my neck off. And look what you've gone and done to my dress. Don't!

– Try to keep calm, Ami my sweet, I say. It'll only take a minute. Then we can put you to bed in that thick tome and in the morning you'll be as fresh as ever and your dress free of all wrinkles. Just give me a couple of seconds, Ami dearest. I know it hurts, but you don't want to stay curled up like this for eternity, do you?

Ami attempts a smile. But it seems to hurts too much and the paper emits a sigh. I shouldn't have come if I had known how much it would hurt. And do you really think it is fun sleeping between the pages of the 1734 edition of the Criminal Code? That is where you intend to put me. Thank you very much indeed.

The pieces of paper rustle almost hysterically. They roll themselves up again and turn their frostbitten, indignant backs on me. I light a cigarette and begin to speak, insistently and pompously, as if addressing a sick person who needs to be convinced to have an operation.

– Don't be so silly, Ami, we'll have to start again now. What's the point of quarrelling when you know all along that this has to be done. Or are you trying to prove that you can hold your own? I know all about that. Do you remember how you once – it must have been a good two years ago – rang me up in the middle of the night and said you were set on going into the countryside to wake up some poor devil. It was Ragnar Ström, who was spending the summer along the coast. I was half asleep and very cross with you, but you succeeded in getting me up and I went outside to look for a cab. Seldom have I sworn as heartily as I did then and, when I subsequently pulled up at your doorstep, furious and drained, you said you'd been waiting for a quarter of an hour already and never thought gentlemen took so long to get dressed. You said it in the calmest tone in the world, as though we were always getting up at 3 o'clock in the morning to drive out to see Ragnar Ström. You just wanted to have your way and maybe, moreover, you thought it was all completely normal. But when, freezing cold and wilting from lack of sleep, we eventually pulled up at his villa, hammered on the door and got him up, you were already so very sleepy you could barely keep your eyes open. You looked so tiny and pale in the morning light and all Ragnar and I could think of was getting you into a bed for some sleep. And I think you yourself felt a bit unhappy about the whole business. But you would not give in at any price and, instead of going to lie down and sleep, you got out Ragnar's entire stock of whisky and sat yourself down on the veranda to drink as the sun came up. It was a magnificent morning, mild and radiantly bright, and the only blot on the horizon was you constantly powdering your nose to mask your washed-out appearance. You looked quite frightful by the end as you sat on the veranda with the rays of the sun playing in your whisky glass and your face chalk-white against the lilac leaves. But you wanted it your way and forced us to drink along and indulge in some of our philosophizing. I think we did so somewhat falteringly and I discovered for the first time that you were actually a little superstitious. You sat there in all seriousness telling ghost stories on a July morning, with the sun laughing and the birds singing, and you did not even notice how grotesque the contrast in mood was. There we sat, Ragnar and I – he in some sort of dressing gown and me in my shirt sleeves – listening to you in amazement. But then we too were seized by a weird feeling in the air, doubtless brought on by the combination of whisky, the summer morning and your deathly pale face framed by the foliage of the lilac tree, and we too began to feel a little creepy. We forgot the sun's rays, the birdsong and the green trees, and started to dig up all sorts of nonsense that we would never have considered mentioning, even at the midnight hour. But here the spooks and visions rose up in glory before our eyes and the smoke from our cigarettes (that morning we puffed away as if there were no tomorrow) coiled mysteriously up into the deep blue sky. It was the most idiotic atmosphere I have ever known; you could call it abnormal, even perverse, but as far as I recall it was entirely respectable. And all because you wanted to have it your way and would not go and lie down for a good sleep.

When we at last packed it in, Ragnar and I had to catch the train to get to work on time and you were absolutely exhausted. We didn't know what the heck to do with you – do you remember, Ami? I doubt you remember anything, actually, because you were too sleepy, although you still somehow had the strength to demand that we stay behind with you and kiss goodbye to our work commitments for the day. We had laid you down in Ragnar's bed (which was three times as big as you) but you would have the last word. You were truly impossible that day.

But when we got back in the afternoon you were all sweetness and light and had turned the kitchen upside down in order to make us something to eat. Do you remember, Ami, how we laughed, Ragnar and I, when we saw your doleful expression as you stood in front of the primus stove, pumping away until your hair fluttered in curls around your head? And when we later moved to the table, you sat there dreamy-eyed and stared out into the garden you had signally failed to notice that morning. I think you were on the verge of feeling ashamed. And when at long last we took the 10 p.m. train into town, you had picked yourself a bunch of flowers to shield you from my possibly somewhat sardonic look. You were so charming and bashful and did not even consider smoking the cigarette I offered you, whilst an elderly lady sat down beside us and covetously observed the skimpy hemline of your skirt. Don't be upset, Ami, I'm only telling you all this so as to remind you how charming and well-behaved you can sometimes be, and how you can put up with rather a lot if you really want something. I'm right, aren't I, Ami? A couple more seconds and I will lay you between pages 201 and 202 in the 1734 Criminal Code and there you can sleep through until the morning and re-emerge as your perky, sweet self.

– The pieces of paper rustle gently and, with a sigh, give in. Good night, Ami, and thank you for your help. We'll continue tomorrow.

V
On hats.

Once we were back in town and elbowing our way through the waiting room, I saw from Ami's face what an irresistible power the city and its atmosphere had over her. The feeble, shy look gradually receded and her eyes regained their hungrily weary gleam. I particularly noticed this as we got into the cab and I was bending over her. A barely discernible and obstinate line had cut into the corners of her mouth and the angle of her head as she leant back in the cab suggested she was striving to hide a level of exertion. She asked the driver take us down the main avenue and her eyes greedily sucked in the frugal lighting which graced the summer evening. She grew more familiar to me again, although - possibly by sheer chance - I positioned myself as far away from her as I could. But once again I felt that unbothered, absolute sense of ownership that we are liable to feel for things so familiar that they are no longer capable of taking us by surprise. I said:

– Surely you must be tired, Ami? Shouldn't we get you home right away? You didn't sleep a wink last night.

She looked up in surprise: – As you wish. Although it's only 10 o'clock. But I don't really mind what we do.

She huddled further into her corner and looked out of the side window. We drove past the harbour, and the skerries sent out their usual friendly twinkle through the heavy, warm air of summer. I still had that same idiotic, self-satisfied feeling of ownership with regard to Ami, and made no effort to get her to turn her head in my direction. She had taken off her hat and was shaking her halo of golden locks. I told the driver to turn round and take us straight to her house.

When we arrived, she got out fast and extended a hand. –

There's no point your following me up, you may as well get straight home if you're so tired. Good night.

As she stood at the door and rummaged for her key, her silhouette blurred somewhat in the white dusk. Her movements were a little too resolute and hurried for someone intending simply to go upstairs to bed. But I never gave the matter a second thought at the time, although in retrospect I find it quite astonishing that I failed to heed those rushed, agitated movements as she opened her handbag and wrestled with the initially unresponsive door.

– I can't quite remember why, but instead of being taken straight home, I ended up at Gunnar's. Probably I happened to catch sight of him in the street and offered him a lift part way, since we were going in the same direction. He was unusually standoffish and curt that evening and the compulsory cigarette bent up challengingly from between his tightened lips. He grimaced when I reported on the previous night's trip to Ragnar's, and the slightly crooked furrow across his brow deepened into a hideous scar. All he said, though, was: were you at work today, by any chance?

– Yes I was, I replied, somewhat offended by his tone, which had a tinge of the accusatory about it. So? Perhaps you phoned while I was out for breakfast... I needed a bit of cheering up today. The bank's food is hardly the perfect hangover cure.

I don't know why I brought out this lengthy excuse, which was all the more unwarranted since I could tell from Gunnar's face that he had not in fact phoned me. My words managed to achieve an effect contrary to that intended; they put up a kind of wall between us, and when I had had my say we both eyed each other with suspicion, as if we could not believe what the other had said. The crease in Gunnar's forehead grew uglier and more scar-like than ever.

– Apparently you just can't let up on this affair, he said in a tone bordering on the menacing. You have stuck with it for over six months and the one visible consequence is that some people have stopped saying hello to you. You must have noticed. Or else you're crazier than I thought.

His voice had grown harsh and jerky. I shrugged my shoulders – basically to hide the fact that he was right. But he was already pacing up and down the low-ceilinged room, with its piles of books and papers, and the sound of his footsteps echoed like drums of war.

– Sorry to keep on at you. You may feel that all I've done lately is nag. But we are friends, for heaven's sake. Can't you see this has to stop? All the mad dashing about and generalized jollification, the chronic hangover you've had for months now. And ultimately I'm to blame for the whole mess, since I introduced you to that – – –. She may well be sweet and nice – and before she chanced upon you, I even found her rather refined and delightful. But she is quite literally driving you crazy, crazy. That's the problem. – He flung his half-smoked cigarette to the floor and frantically lit another. The scar on his forehead resembled an open wound.

I shrugged my shoulders again. I was used to this kind of thing from Gunnar – and anyway, I of all people knew how right he was. His sermons were pretty harmless, anyway; once he had let off steam, he became the nicest chap in the world. Meanwhile the storm raged on.

– Do you know what I heard today when I was up in the editorial office? Looks like the game may well be up for you in a year's time. Where the hell do you think you're going to get the money from for all this carrying on? You've got away with it so far, fair enough. The banks are still giving you credit and your cement dealings have so far paid for wining and dining Ami. But do you seriously believe they're going to keep on building houses for ever and a day in Helsinki? You're an idiot! – he lit another cigarette. The word 'idiot' had clearly brought some release. His tie had loosened and the knot widened.

What's the real state of play with that last consignment? he asked, in somewhat milder, yet at the same time more suspicious tone. It should surely be here any day now.

– The bill of lading's being called in, I replied, and he started as if stung by a wasp. –Just as I thought, damn it! So – and he stood in front of me, his hands in his trouser pockets, his

26

cigarette almost vertical. So, what on earth are you proposing to do now?

– I paid a visit to the bank today, I answered, possibly somewhat evasively. It'll be fine.

But this was a man intent on a true cross-examination. How much?

– 11. – I was beginning to get angry.

– How long?

– 2 months.

– Have you spoken to Stenberg?

– Yes.

– What did he say?

– That he'd let me know tomorrow.

– He turned abruptly on his heels and a pile of newspapers collapsed on to the floor. He gave them a kick.

– It was Stenberg I saw in the editorial office today, he said quietly after a short pause. He said – – well, you know what he said. – –

Although I could well imagine the conversation in question, I was unable to hide my curiosity: Go on, what did he say?

– That the time is nigh, dear friend – Gunnar addressed the bookshelf opposite me. That you might, if you're lucky – if you're lucky – hang on until the autumn. Then – – he clearly did not want to give away something he had been asked to keep quiet about. But I was not going to let him off the hook now: then the banks will withdraw the building loan, I proffered casually, and anxiously observed his averted head.

Precisely – his cigarette shot across the room like a rocket. In the autumn the game will be up with your cement. That's what Stenberg said.

– Autumn's a long way off, I ventured foolishly. And anyway, Sternberg has spent his whole life predicting financial crises. – – I had dropped another clanger and hung my head in shame. –

Gunnar by now had sat down on the chair opposite me. He had sunk forward and his affable eyes peered out, ready to pounce from beneath the scar on his forehead (which still did not seem to want to go away). He wearily shrugged his shoulders

– Sorry for having a go at you rather than offering more practical assistance. But what is one to do with a gent like you? – Who just doesn't get it – – Who is plain crazy. – Who embarks on excursions to the country in the middle of the night and raises a glass as the sun goes up. How can a chap not have a go?

We both attempted a laugh. It wasn't very convincing, but it was better than nothing: I said

– If that business with Stenberg gets sorted out tomorrow, we'll go and have dinner somewhere. How does that sound?

– Will Ami be coming with us? he hastily enquired and his cigarette bobbed in the air. In which case – –

– No, she won't be coming with us, I said reassuringly, and immediately regretted my words – – Highly unlikely, unless she phones to say she has nothing in to eat. She occasionally does. – – But I don't think she will – – at any rate, I'll try to avert such an eventuality. If that's what you want.

He laughed out loud. It sounded as forced as before, and perhaps cost him more effort than ever: if that's what I want. His cigarette shot across the room again and expired slowly and reluctantly in a corner. If that's what I want? Well, well, I really do hope to have the pleasure of Ami's company tomorrow. But now it's time for you to go home. You didn't sleep a wink last night.

– That's true, I remembered, and felt an urgent need to be on my way. It's nearly one and I have to be bright and breezy and confidence-inspiring when I go up to see Stenberg tomorrow morning. Good night.

– The summer air was as heavily grey and warm as earlier on in the evening. The light over the skerries had grown paler, but went on sending its friendly, panting greetings across the water. After the cigarette smoke in Gunnar's room, it was good to bathe one's face in the mild, pure breeze coming off the sea. I didn't go straight home, but instead made a brief diversion and just happened to pass by the house where Ami lived.

I should probably never have noticed her window had a light on had not all the others been sunk in deep, sleeping darkness. I became aware of this well before I reached her house, but the thought that it must have been her window only hit home much later, once I was already a fair way along the street. It hit home so suddenly that I did not initially grasp my potential personal involvement. My only thought was: hmm, she's not in bed yet, she must still have had something to do this evening. And my absolute sense of possession of her, quite possibly stemming from sheer tiredness, meant that I was momentarily incapable of imagining what she might conceivably have to do in her own home at one o'clock in the morning, I thought: it must be the wrong window, not hers. She'll have been asleep for ages now.

I walked on in mechanical fashion, but my footsteps began to drag and eventually came to a total halt. Was it Ami's window I had been looking at, or something else? This thought, which had initially involved no more than an objective examination of the phenomenon, subsequently merged with a continually growing interest as to what Ami could possibly be doing so late at night. I slowly went back. Her house was already discernible, and I eagerly sought, but failed to locate, the illuminated window. I was looking throughout at her second-floor window and nearly crashed into a man who was hurriedly coming across the street. He muttered an apology and rushed on and I could now pick out Ami's window. It was buried in the heavy grey dawn of the summer's night, just like all the others.

But as I was walking home a sick feeling began to well up inside me. I didn't yet know exactly what it was, for it was thus far too amorphous to form into a specific thought or sensation. – – Had I seen a light in Ami's window or not? And if her light was indeed on, what could she have been doing at this time of night? For that matter, what could Ami conceivably be doing anyway? I had never seen her do more than put on a gramophone record or flick through film magazines when she was at home. – She admittedly picked up some needlework now and then, but she never completed whatever it was. – – A cushion or such like. She said it was a piece of embroidery – with birds of paradise or parrots – although the names of the birds kept changing. For heaven's sake, though, she was surely not going to sit and embroider parrots in the middle of the night? That was really just too ridiculous – and perhaps it hadn't been her window anyway. In which case the birds of paradise and so on were beside the point. – I switched off the lamp and turned resolutely to the wall: any minute now and I'd be asleep. – But what if it had been her window after all. – – A chap had brushed past me outside her front door. He had apologized and raised, or rather touched, his hat. It was grey, with the brim turned down at the front. Who might he be? Tall, with a tightly fitting overcoat and a grey summer hat with the front brim down.

And suddenly I sat up in bed and let out a frenzied laugh into the murky room; I had a hat just like that myself! Pale grey, with the front brim turned down and an even paler band than his! Ha ha ha, he and I had the same hat, we did. If he got it at Stockmann's it would have cost him 140 Marks. Ha ha ha! Would Ami have spotted that? Of course she would, she adored trying on hats, men's in particular. She would have stood in front of the mirror, with him so close behind her that she needed to lean forward to get it on. And then – – she had swung round and commandingly lifted her lips to his face, or else flopped back, as was her wont. – – All the while wearing a hat that looked just like mine. Ha ha ha.

– The room listened, surprised, and the furniture, in particular the desk and the bookshelves, assumed a shocked expression. I suddenly began to feel embarrassed in their presence. – I had after all gone to bed in order to sleep –. And tomorrow – hell's teeth, tomorrow Stenberg would be passing his verdict. What sort of hat did Stenberg wear? A bowler? But not always. Sometimes he sported a – pale grey felt hat with – – the brim turned up. Turned up – – and with a black band. Am I right about that? I'll have to check what sort of hat Stenberg wears tomorrow. But there was the matter of the turned up brim – – –

VI

28438   – Hello, is that Ami?
– A yawn.
– Morning, Ami, not awake yet?
– No.
– So you didn't you go straight to bed when you got home yesterday?
– Yes I did.
– But I walked past around one o'clock and thought there was a light on in your window.
– Silence.
– Hello?
– Must have forgotten to turn off the light when I settled down to sleep – – I did a little reading before dropping off – – Forgot to turn off the light.
– Ami, do you think a pale grey hat suits a man? You see, I left mine in the cab yesterday evening and cannot recall the driver's number. Shall I buy myself another one?
– Down goes the receiver.
53066   – Trrrr.
– Good morning, Mr Stenberg, Sir. How kind of you to ring so early. I was just about to ring you myself.
– It's about that matter the gentleman raised yesterday. I was thinking it over last night.
– You were...
– I will oblige if a second person offers to stand surety.
– Do you think that is absolutely necessary?

– I certainly do. And one further point. Definitely no more renewals. If the gentleman cares to call in after one o'clock we can make the arrangements. Your bank is KOP, isn't it?

– Thank you, Sir, I will be there. It is indeed KOP. Goodbye.

Down goes the receiver.

10537   – Morning Sven, Henry here. Listen, I need to ask you a small favour. Do you have any stock in KOP?

– A fair bit. Why?

– I'm going to need a second person to stand surety.

– Who's the other one?

– Stenberg.

– Won't his name do on its own?

– You know him, he likes to be difficult. He wants two standing surety. But it's a pure formality. Can you oblige?

– How much?

– 11.

– Well, well. We're playing for high stakes, aren't we? But – – why not? If Stenberg's on board. – –

– I'll be up to see you at half past twelve. Bye for now.

– Down goes the receiver.

4456   – Morning, Gunnar, it's Henry. We're back in business. Where shall we go for dinner?

– You mean to say you pulled it off? Well done old fellow. And sorry about yesterday. I – –

– Oh, don't worry. Stenberg wanted a second person to stand surety and good old Sven said he'd do it. Not bad, eh? I might ask him along if that's all right with you. How about the Palladium? We can meet there at five o'clock.

– Will Ami be coming?

– No she won't. Tell me, do you think you can

recognise a chap if you know he has a pale grey summer hat with the front brim turned down? Like mine – –

– Down goes the receiver.

VII

– I played cards yesterday, says Ami. I began by winning 160 Marks, but that went faster than it had come. All the same, it was fun.

– How much? I ask as calmly as possible, reaching prematurely for my breast pocket.

But Ami pretends not to hear what I am saying. Perhaps she really cannot hear. Her hands are pressed against her curls as she watches the seagulls wheeling up and down in front of the café terrace. She looks small and dreamy.

– How much? I repeat. I'm a little edgy now. 200? 300? 500? 1000? Tell me.

But she just sits there pressing her head between her fingers so that the curls push out through the gaps. She then turns towards me and I can see clearly from her face that she really hasn't understood what I said. The smile is addressed to herself alone and there is no sign of any awareness that I am sitting there next to her.

– Do you think it would be difficult to drown yourself here? she asks after a while, facing the seagulls once more. They glide encouragingly by on their glittering white wings and one plummets headlong into the water: it's that simple. Comes up again and sails disdainfully on, followed by the others.

– How much? I repeat so firmly that, this time, she can't avoid hearing. 2000? You truly got yourself in the soup yesterday. Come on, out with it, for heaven's sake.

She turns swiftly towards me and she has the eyes of a wounded beast: what exactly do you want of me? Fifty Marks. Seventy-five if you must know. And that of course is why I want to drown myself. Eh? She laughs, and her voice is piercing and shrill like the shrieks of the gulls.

 – What's the problem? I ask, puzzled. Something rustles between my fingers and I shamefacedly stuff the notes back in my pocket. Hell, why does one always rush into these things?

Ami gives me a spiteful look. What's the problem? You, and you alone. I am sick to the teeth of you. And I cannot escape you. It is my supreme privilege to sit here beside you and watch you drink your coffee. Once you've finished your cup, you will proceed to allow me the honour of pouring you another one. Isn't that enough?

 – My darling little Ami, I respond, in as friendly a tone as I can. You need not pour me another coffee if it upsets you. I can easily do it myself. – – But I break off in dismay. She is lying prostrate across the table, sobbing and sobbing. Thank goodness there is no one nearby.

Then she sits up with a jolt and falls on to my shoulder. A waitress appears briefly, but withdraws again in dismay. It really is a stroke of luck that there is no one else in the seafront café. Fortunately it is dinner time – – For Ami is still sobbing uncontrollably and here am I in the most ridiculous situation I've ever been in my life, holding my breath and listening out for footsteps. – – Please, don't let anyone come. What the devil has got into the girl? Has she rekindled an old acquaintance? – – She used to get like this afterwards at times like that – – Or have I really wounded her with my questions? I honestly didn't know she was so touchy. Lord above, please don't let anyone come.

There is nothing more awkward for a man – I think I'm entitled to generalise here – than to be sitting on a chair with a girl sobbing against his shoulder. You feel in such instances like a piece of old furniture, the arm of a chair or something and, in a matter of minutes, you actually become as stiff as wood and quite indifferent; you sit there and tense the muscles in your back so as not to sag under the weight and you think about this, that or the other, but definitely not about the tiny heap of misery next to you, which happens to be one hundred percent convinced that you are compassion and consolation incarnate. With your conscious brain unengaged, you pass a gentle-mechanical hand over her hair, mutter a trite banality and your thoughts wander off goodness knows where. And likewise now: when Ami - after what seemed to me a truly incomprehensible outburst of hysteria - all of a sudden sought my support, she actually drove my emotions in an entirely different direction. For whilst she was lolling there on my shoulder and I, in seemingly gentle and encouraging fashion, stroked the back of her neck, my mind was positively not engaged in suppositions as to the cause of her despair; instead I was busy thinking about a letter I had received that morning, which involved Ami only to the extent that it held out the prospect of a pretty profitable deal.

I thought about the letter and the possibilities it opened up with regard to my recently very grave financial situation and concluded that here was a potential way out. Not cement this time, but a delivery of sheet metal, which - if the deal went through - would do more for my disquieting financial situation than I had recognized when first reading the letter. And as I sat there, mechanically stroking Ami's neck and hair, a plan took shape all of a sudden, a plan so simple and, to my mind, so utterly inspired that I just knew the deal would succeed, thus putting an end to all my cares and troubles. It simply had to go through! The brilliance of the plan lay in its capacity to deposit all my competitors in a subordinate category, with me - so to speak - surging forward as leader of the pack. And my hands, infected by this unbridled explosion of innermost joy, which swept away my worries of yore, at once sensed victory and glided ever more nimbly and triumphantly over Ami's sobbing locks, with the result that she pressed even closer against me and appeared to calm down. At least I assume that's what happened, for while I was busy rocking her into a state of peaceful lethargy (all of this performed in purely mechanical, or at least unpremeditated fashion) I continued to adorn my plan with assorted details and options, a process which poured new strength into the benumbed muscles of my back; and I must have sat supporting Ami on my left shoulder for around half an hour without experiencing the slightest fatigue.

But in the end, once every last detail of the plan destined to lead to my resurrection was in place, and I had even managed to think out a reply to the lucky letter, my thoughts began tentatively to feel their way back to the starting point, and I became aware once more of Ami sitting next to me. She had straightened herself up somewhat and was no longer slumped in quite so prostrate a fashion against my shoulder, which now really was turning numb. Initially I gave a slight start, since I thought she might have noticed my indifference towards her at that particular moment, but then I discovered she was holding my hand in hers and, when she turned her head towards me, a still slightly moist gleam was shimmering in her eyes and begging for forgiveness. I endeavoured to adjust as fast as I could to the new situation and harnessed all of my energy in a bid to drive out my all-consuming obsession with the projected letter. Now I needed to prepare myself to hear Ami's confession or, at any rate, an explanation for her strange behaviour. She was gazing at me in such a beseeching way, and looked so fragile and tiny, that I actually managed, with desperate endeavour, to lock away my obsessive (and, to me, infinitely seductive) thoughts into a rear compartment of my brain. I leaned closer and stroked her hand.

– My darling little Ami, I said. There was a certain afterglow of victory in my voice, which I quickly sensed and suppressed. How's my girl feeling now? Perhaps you needed a good cry. Luckily there was nobody around to see, so no damage has been done whatsoever.

– A barely perceptible shadow of surprise passed over Ami's mild, affable face. She cast a swift glance around her and I'm convinced that only now did she realize that we were on the terrace of a seafront café and not in her room. But then the remorseful expression was back in all its glory:

– I'm sorry – to make such a fuss, – – and in such a public place, she said softly. But I get overcome on occasions. And then I just can't take it anymore. – –

– What can't you take any more? I asked, mystified.

She looked up in surprise: – All this – –. Having sold myself to you – –. But I haven't sold myself to you, she sniffed with a returning sob. – I bet you think I have though.

37

– Hmm, I could not help myself from saying, but I don't think she heard. To this day I hope you did not hear, Ami. – I said:

– Where in heaven's name did you get that idea from? Why should I think such a crazy thought? We're friends, aren't we?

Perhaps, she murmured even more softly. But you sounded so dreadfully businesslike when I was telling you about the game of cards. It really hurt – –

I honesty didn't know what to say. But she cuddled up closer and raised her face to mine. Kiss me, she commanded in timid, yet firm fashion.

I looked apprehensively around me. The waitress was standing nearby, looking on with unabashed interest; at which point I made the mightiest sacrifice I ever made for Ami. I cast a pleading look in the direction of the waitress, leant down and kissed Ami on the mouth.

VIII

A few days later Ami came up to the office and I sensed right away from her expression that she had something important to say. She entered in her nonchalant, slightly bowed way – a posture that made her look smaller than she really was. Sank into the chair that had been put out for visitors, my hat clasped in her hands. How she got hold of it, heaven only knows, but she proceeded to turn and inspect it before casting it abruptly aside.

Her eyes soon began to veer towards the half-open door leading to the outer room, where the intermittent clatter of typewriters suggested in a discreet, yet emphatic way that 'Parland and Co.' was never short of work. (Actually, the staff had been instructed to beaver away like mad whenever a visitor worthy of impressing came into the office. Seemingly Ami had been erroneously placed in this category.) I casually remarked in a tone of indifference that she was looking unusually spruce today, but by then her preparation phase was over and she launched into her question: do you think you could afford another typist?

What's that supposed to mean? I said, flabbergasted, and tried in vain to guess what might follow after such an original introduction.

– I've been thinking about applying for a position, Ami replied calmly and looked me straight in the eye.

Some time must have passed before I answered, but when I finally managed to pull myself together, I burst out laughing. She eyed me with reproach.

– What on earth has got into you, Ami? Are you unwell? Or – – surely you haven't been drinking today?

She picked up my hat again and inspected it closely: why – –

– why do you speak to me like that? You don't seem to understand – that I want to put an end to this way of carrying on. Why shouldn't I work and earn money just like anyone else?

– But that's precisely the point, I interjected. You cannot work and earn money like anyone else. It wouldn't suit you. It – would spoil your hands, dear Ami, don't look so crestfallen. I'm so sorry, you'd be great at anything else – but work: no.

Normally Ami would have thrown something at me after a reply like that. But she began to cry – Lord above, how often she had cried recently, and so inopportunely! Perhaps I should have questioned her more closely first – it was after all just another of her bright ideas, to be handled with care. Perhaps I should have behaved with greater circumspection. Unless she really was short of money. But the girl had recently become so impossible that I was afraid to risk that question right now.

She sat there in the chair meant for rich, rotund businessmen and gently blew her nose into a handkerchief too drenched in perfume for drying away tears. Squeezed in the palm of one of her hands was my hat, its turned down brim running a serious risk of becoming turned up. As soon as the aforementioned deal went through I really should buy myself a new one. – This particular model had cost 140 Marks – at Stockmann's. Or was it the hat of the man I had met that night whose hat was worth 140? Just a minute, how could I have known how much his hat cost? Silly me: because we both had the same hat of course. – Was it perhaps his hat that Ami was currently holding in her hand? – – Hell, surely not, how could that fellow's hat have got here? (Just to be on the safe side I glanced over at the coat-stand by the door and there was nothing on it.) Of course it was my hat that Ami was doing her best to destroy. But that man – – and again my thoughts strayed from Ami's trials and tribulations, yet resistance met them on all fronts and they were obliged to return to the hat, around which they began to circle at ever-increasing speed.

– It's strange, but each time I try to cast myself back to the period before Ami's death, the best way is to take as my starting point that hat which one night drifted past me and, even today, will not let me alone. It is frankly hard to explain why an insignificant – and, thanks to the summer dawn, somewhat blurred circumstance, to which I attached no importance at the time, should have eaten into my memory in such unyielding and relentless fashion. Possibly it has to do partly with the fact that, soon afterwards, I lost my mastery of Ami, so that this was effectively the last time she could cheat on me. But I don't believe this explanation tells the whole story. It is instead a construct, put in place much later, which therefore in no way offers a key to why, just hours after that meeting, I began to be persecuted by some kind of *idée fixe*, with which I created permanent and unyielding torment not only for myself, but also, given the inveigling nature of my suspicion, for Ami too. On the other hand, it cannot be denied that this *idée fixe* is proving, and will continue to prove, of considerable value in the writing of this book.

For there are evenings when it is clearly Ami who is in a foul mood and her photograph takes on a bored, indifferent expression. And on such occasions I'd be incapable of writing a single word if I didn't have that unfortunate hat. All I then need to do (much to my dismay, since anxiety and ill-humour are basically all that ensue) is to conjure up the hat up as clearly I can: and immediately I have before me the balmy summer street and a big, unyielding five-storey block with dead windows. And I even find acoustic images popping into my consciousness, the sound of steps hastily and softly padding the pavement (he obviously must have had rubber heels) and suddenly growing silent at the crossroads. And if, ignoring the anxious feeling that always grabs me by the scruff of the neck when I let the memory in, I dwell on it for a moment instead and let it expand to fill the full space of my imagination, the shutter-like structures in my consciousness suddenly slide aside as I, unimpeded, move among the events of that summer. All I need do now is bend down and pick up one situation or another from the ground to feel how it wriggles through my fingers and then, with some reluctance, eventually settles down submissively on the pages of this book. – But, as I said, I'm not too happy doing this, since it's always connected with a whole mass of uncomfortable associations and thoughts, which plague me long into the night and won't leave me alone even as I sleep. The morning is then well-advanced when I awake and I have to dress in a great hurry if I am to get to the consulate on time to do what has to be done. And while I am getting dressed, all sorts of vague memories of the dreams of the night before well up inside me and only settle down once I am launched into my work, which I perform with special fervour on days like this. In self-defence.

– I actually think it was on the precise day that Ami came and asked me to procure her a position that this particular madness finally took hold of me. Somehow it was her look as she sat there, one minute sobbing, the next drying her eyes and casting me furtive, pleading glances - which I did not notice, since the poison was already in my body, thus speeding up the disease process no end. There was a marked sense of contrast in the situation (just as I had experienced at Ragnar's in the morning) and this fired my imagination, conjuring up some huge, ghoulish vision. In the end, all I could see was Ami and the hat, which she held in her hand, while the walls of the room, the typewriters, the desk, all slipped away into the blue yonder, abandoning me to my *idée fixe*, which nosed its way in the direction of my heart.
– – – Why hadn't she given me an answer when I questioned her on the phone the following morning? Of course she felt guilty; if she hadn't understood when I asked her why she hadn't answered she could easily have asked what I meant. After all, she loved spending hours on the phone. But she had simply not been prepared when I rang and woke her up, so she had simply hung up in order to win time to invent a good lie. – – And now she turned up here and played all innocent – she wanted to get a job. – Did she honestly think I'd fall for that one? And look at her pretending to cry. I think she even managed a real tear. – – Sorry, but it's high time to say what I have to say. – And what on earth is she doing with that hat in her hand? For heaven's sake, it's mine not his – –

It was more a reflex action triggered by this latter thought than any intended rudeness that made me snatch the hat from her hand and throw it up on to the bookshelf. She gave a start and looked at me with sadness and incomprehension. Her face really did look as if she had been crying and, as she began – at first uncomprehendingly and then with clear disgust – to decipher the expression on my face, she curled up in a corner of the huge armchair like a dog who knows that it is about to get a beating, but cannot quite remember what it has done wrong.

– Listen, Ami, I said, stop this endless howling, which is beginning to get to me. And before we discuss your business further, perhaps you would be so kind as to answer a couple of questions I'd like to put to you. Stay in your seat! – she had half stood up and seemed on the verge of departing. – How about a cigarette?

She tentatively reached out for one, but her face had meanwhile taken on that hard, defiant expression she always adopted as a defence on such occasions. I realized I had not exactly chosen the ideal moment to force a confession, but my jealousy was too far advanced for me to stop now.

– Perhaps you'd care to tell me what you got up to that evening after we came back from Ragnar's. When I walked past your window there was a light on at one o'clock in the morning. Who did you have up there with you?

– She gestured impatiently. – But I've already – –

– You're a liar.

– She screwed up her eyes and a weary, vampish line cut across the corners of her mouth. I'd seen this look before, having frequently observed it in the early days of our acquaintance when she was still mixing with her old friends.

– I want to know who was there with you. –

– She leapt up from the chair, placed her hands on her hips, and her shrill, hate-filled laugh hit me in the face:

– A man, with a grey hat just like yours. But that, I assure you, is the only similarity between you. Because you are a lowly beast!

Luckily, the weightiest object I had to hand was the blotter and it ended up smashing against the door that Ami had already slammed behind her.

IX
I take fright.

The period immediately following that office incident is one of the hardest for me to think myself back into. I frankly cannot remember any real facts whatsoever from that time, and it is perfectly possible that nothing very special or noteworthy occurred. It is as if some kind of heavy, grey haze, in which small specks of light – *mouches volantes* – ceaselessly drift, had settled over those days, and from within its vagueness visual images leap out, flare up for a fraction of a second and encourage me, with their magnesium light, to behold all sorts of non-existent things. In order to characterise that period in my life, which probably lasted no longer than a week and left me with nothing but an unreal, almost indefinable impression, the answer is probably to catch those flashes at the very moment they resurface and not to let them go until they have been committed to paper, thereby taking on material form and – becoming simply ordinary. For I, at any rate, always feel that I am committing sacrilege whenever I start sounding the depths of my unconscious, hauling out those wondrous deepwater fish we normally explain away as hallucinations, dreams, etc. And when such a fantastical beast, after a long and sometimes forlorn wait, at long last takes the hook, swollen with the most appetizing, wriggling associations, it is not enough just to draw in the line; no, at that very instant, the brain needs to work with supreme precision, taking an instant snapshot of the beast, developing it and fixing it on paper. For just as deepwater fish, no sooner have they been pulled from their element, metamorphoze into formless, dead lumps of jelly as the unaccustomed air pressure at the sea's surface smashes them into pieces, so those previous representations fall apart as soon as they reach the light of day.

Angling is a trying sport. And I have often waited for hours, staring at the occasionally quivering surface of my consciousness, the float only ever moving by accident, nudged by the wind, or upended by a wave from who knows where. You sit there and see shadows and shivers glide over the water, you sometimes even think there is a tug on the float and you wait with bated breath, expecting to see it dive under and disappear. But usually this is only an illusion, or else some silly insignificant thought has begun to chew at the association you cast out, and when you come to pull in the line the bait has gone and the harsh gleam of the hook has chased away the elusive, deepwater fish. There is nothing more irritating than those silly little thoughts, they sometimes come in dense swarms and the water gleams with the spinning and splashing of their tails. You eventually have to up sticks and move farther down the beach so as to recast your line and resume your numbing contemplation of the bobbing float. At which point you are liable to experience the same disillusion as before: the small fish merrily snap up the bait, only to rise to the surface to sun themselves and chase away the specks of dust that have settled upon them. You bank on the most juicy and untrammelled association, it swims circles here, there and everywhere and, with a protestation, disappears into the deep. Shadows and shivers glide over the water. You are by now tired of all the waiting, you are even a little sleepy and you begin to doze, with the sunny wiles of those small thoughts still playing in your eyes. You forget the float, which the breeze has sent somewhat to the side, the nervous tension gradually lets go and your breathing becomes regular and calm. When all of a sudden some new perception glides across your retina: the shadow of a water ring as it hits the shore, causing you to come to with a jerk. You look around uncomprehendingly; you discover all of a sudden that the float is no longer visible and you hear instead the sound of ever more ripples as they splash gently against the shore. You pull in the rod, it bends like a bow, the line is taut as a violin string and now – – now the fabulous beast rears up, shimmering in all the colours of the rainbow as it flies in a wide arch over your head and drops down upon the flat rocks behind you.

But your brain, if it is a skilful photographer and has already attempted such shots before, has meanwhile been madly cranking itself up so as to catch the magical fish in mid-flight. For the brain knows that this fabulous gaping mouth and tiny tail, or else this magical splurge of colour - which proffers you a moment of bliss, since it and it alone can open the gates of the paradise of your dreams - will, as soon as it hits the earth, metamorphoze into a mass of shivering jelly: a substance that may well hold out some interest for scholars of deepwater fish, but is as irrelevant to that magnificent being momentarily hovering over our heads as a book on the interpretation of dreams is to our innermost visions.

Among the strange beings I manage to drag up from the deepest layers of my subconscious is one I have often felt snap at the hook, but it always gets away just when I think I am ready to bring my precious catch safely to land. And although I possess not a single solid image of it, and suspect I never will, I do know that it is in fact that fabulous black-scaled beast who circled around me during those nights and night-like days after Ami had walked away and closed the office door behind her. I cannot describe this beast, nor even visualize it in my imagination, but I do know that it had a mouth studded with crooked, spiky teeth and a powerful, irregularly-shaped tail which propelled it through the dark and gave me the odd little prod. And it was generally at just such a moment that the unsettling and stifling vision rose up within me.

But when I eventually managed to get to sleep, another being came to me, so resplendent in its display of colour that the fabulous black beast was no match. It vanished and my dreams were lit by a still, muted glow as the dark figures gradually ceded their place to figures of pale brightness. And, emerging from the shadow dance of these bright, pale beings, one figure came forward to my bed and I knew that it was Ami, although she had a different face and a different name and was forever changing shape. She would come towards me in the street, sometimes she simply sat down beside me and all of a sudden I remembered that

46

she had already been sitting there for a long, long time, leaning ever closer, and all I needed to do was reach out a hand in order to touch her. Then I forgot about her again, but the glow emanating from her went on warming my heart and I entered a restaurant where Ami was dancing with a strange man - who was, I knew, my brother. What I really mean is: possibly it was Ami and, casting myself back into that situation, I can see that she had Ami's features, but I did not recognize her just then and felt total indifference towards her.

X

The conclusion to this story is equally unclear and unreal to me. That day, framed in a dank, autumnal atmosphere, could perhaps best be compared to the first symptoms of awakening after a nightmare, as the meagre, grey daylight sifts into the room through the drawn curtains and is yet too weak to fight off the ghostly figures crowding around the bed. If my memory serves me well, I got up unusually late on that particular day and was in such a rush to get to the office in time that I did not give Ami a thought. It was only later, whilst looking up a number in the telephone book, that I chanced upon the name of the street where she lived and that was all it took – after half an hour's prevarication, during which I got through half a packet of cigarettes – to get me to ring up Ami; only to hear that she had gone out, but that, if I wished to speak to her, I could see her at 6 o'clock.

I must have behaved with unusual courtesy and correctness as I spoke to the maid, but no sooner had she put down the receiver than something unpleasant began to well up inside me. I stood up, put on my hat and coat and shot out of the office without even bothering to tidy away the papers on the desk in front of me. Even while I was still talking to the maid, I had kept looking at the clock and worked out that, given it was now 12.30, I had five and a half hours to go before I would see Ami. But once out in the street, I had already forgotten and had to look again and I did so over and over as I wandered aimlessly from café to café, running into acquaintances and exchanging a few words. I suddenly found myself sitting at one of their tables, an untouched cup of coffee in front of me, glanced briefly at my watch, which had moved on ten minutes since I last looked, rushed off in the sort of state a chap can get into when he has an important meeting to attend and is not yet sure that he will make it on time. My watch meanwhile crawled along with a merciless disregard for speed. I sometimes thought it had stopped altogether and, quaking with hope, held it up to my ear: perhaps the time really was later than it said. But again came the calm, ironic tick tock and I could see that the second hand was indeed creeping forward, only it had hidden for a while under the minute hand and was now emerging, full of *schadenfreude*, from its hiding place, torturing me to death as it tripped past each little black line.

It is strange how, ever since that moment when I dialled Ami's number, all my indelible resolutions never again to exchange a word with her, and preferably never even to think of her, suddenly vanished, so that for five and a half hours I harboured not a single doubt as to whether or not to try to see her. Of course I would be there. I don't think that anything in the world could have stopped me; I should have laughed in the face of any lunatic who might have suggested I would not be there at the foreseen time. The decision I had taken – or, more accurately, the decision that had seized me by the throat – seemed to me as obvious as electing to strike the end of a match with a head, rather than the one without, against a matchbox. And Ami, who undoubtedly knew me well, had presumably reckoned with my change of heart anyway, since the order passed on to me by her maid had no doubt been issued several days previously and Ami couldn't reasonably have known when my change of heart would occur. That she knew it would occur sooner or later is proven by the maid's tone of voice, which betrayed not the slightest surprise, but rather rattled off what she had learnt with the aplomb of someone who had been primed to answer the question for days. My extraordinary agitation throughout those many hours, as I dashed up and down streets like some kind of maniac, was therefore in no way triggered by any hesitation or inner conflict (that had ceased as soon as I placed my finger in the hole corresponding to the first digit of her number on the telephone dial); instead what drove me on was a blind impatience to see

Ami, even if just for a moment, and to hell with the consequences. The fact is that I had so thoroughly succumbed to the power of my own impatience, which blotted out all thought, that it was not until I was standing in front of Ami's door a few minutes before 6 that I was able to give the situation any real consideration. My thought process, however, lasted but a moment; once I was in the hallway, mechanically examining my face in the mirror, my brain was as empty of thought as earlier in the day, and I simply strode into the room where Ami was sitting, driven solely by the aforesaid agitation, which nonetheless waned with every step and was gradually replaced by a terrible sense of fatigue and unease.

She plainly noticed how unprepared and feeble I was at that moment and therefore switched straight to the offensive. She did so very skilfully, asked me to take a seat, reached out a hand and said: Well, well, so at long last we're getting to see you again. It has been a while – –

She very skilfully checked the triumph that was seeping through between her words, thereby avoiding the risk of any destabilizing outburst on my part. I simply said: yes, it has been a while. I happened to ring you up today and was told you wished to speak to me.

– Have a chair and take off your coat.

Getting out of the coat was a struggle. Fatigue descended upon my limbs like lead, and I collapsed into an available chair, helpless and feeling an irresistible desire to slump against Ami's shoulder and rest.

She came over to my chair and sat on the arm. So here you are again, she said, pensively, pulling down her skirt which had ridden up over her knees.

I said nothing in reply. She was so right, damn it. Here I was again, and that was basically the end of it. Did I maybe have something to add? In a half motherly, half ironic way, Ami bent over me. And I cuddled up closer to the warmth and felt like a puppy who had at last found a snug spot in front of the fire.

XI

From that day forward, I steered clear of Ami. I only ever saw her by accident and we might on occasion end up sitting in the same café at separate tables. She was usually with a party of some kind – people I barely knew – and I would shelter behind a newspaper or else nod in such a way as to signal that I was momentarily preoccupied with other things. Sometimes Ami would then come over for a couple of minutes, but she never even sat down; instead we exchanged a few clumsy, inept words and then her coat confidently and coolly swished past the table and back to her companions. Whilst I lit a cigarette and felt a lump of lead forming inside me.

It was as if something holding us together us had fallen to pieces on the afternoon I tried to thaw my frozen love with warmth from Ami's neckline. For when, after half an hour or so, I wakened from that particular fatigue which had cast me prostrate on a chair in her room, we looked at one another like strangers do when they have behaved in an unconventional fashion: embarrassed, yet determined to get out of their predicament. Ami's fingers, which had burrowed into my hair, were suddenly lying against my head like stiff wooden pegs and I sensed she was fighting an urge to pull them away. We hurriedly put on our outdoor clothes and went to the pictures. And as we sat pressed up close, each of us longed to be sitting in another row, or with at least two seats between us to give us some breathing space.

It's quite likely that I was rather unsociable during that period. I went about and felt a lump of lead increasing in size within me. It weighed down my step and I would on occasions sit for hours in a café without the energy to pay my bill and go. Perhaps I was waiting for Ami to come in with her companion and sit down at the next table. For I recall that I was forever looking towards the door and searching among the people coming in, my heart in my throat. But if Ami actually came in, I dug myself in behind the newspaper (procured in advance to this very end) and barely looked up to greet her and her retinue.

After which I sat back and enjoyed a few moments of calm. She was within reach – third table to the left – and I knew that three or four steps would take me there. And that was enough for me. If I wished I could go and join them, and therefore I stayed put. Now and then, from beneath the newspaper, I cast a covert, sweeping look around the whole room and, as it passed across Ami's table, I saw that she had begun to wear more face powder again and noticed that her face had grown older and wearier over the past months. I logged this with indifferent callousness and bent over the newspaper – only to take another covert glance over the top and turn away, abashed, if she happened to turn her head in my direction.

One day we happened to arrive at the restaurant at the same time. I only realized when we both found ourselves in front of the cloakroom mirror, applying the final touches to our appearances before going in. Ami was slightly in front of me and her head, which I could see in the mirror, gave a surprised twist by way of a greeting.

– Do I look dreadful? she asked my reflection, forcing the comb through her as always somewhat ruffled locks. I really am so tired today. The comb had slid out of her curls and they sighed gently.

– Perhaps you do look a little tired, I said. But frankly you often are.

I should never have dared say that right to her face, but I could risk it with the mirror there. It cast back a smile, which got swallowed by the hallway behind my back.

– Why do we see you so seldom these days? – she asked after a while and turned towards me. And, putting the comb in her handbag, she edged really close.

I waved my arm in a manner intended to make clear that I had a lot on my plate and would prefer not to pursue the matter. But, with her standing so close, my arm collided with hers, giving the impression that I had wanted to push her away. She looked reproachfully up at me, yet came even closer.

– Can't you sit with me for a bit? My friends are already in there, but I don't feel like going to join them right away. They are so boring – –.

– So am I, I said, but it sounded apologetic. I was speaking as we were already going through the door into the main restaurant area and it was therefore too late to adjust my tone.

Anyone coming into a restaurant always feels a bit bewildered at the beginning: all those tables to choose from, so many hostile eyes homing in and giving advance notice of disapproval. A person coming into a restaurant is viewed by those who have already been seated at their tables for ten minutes as a greenhorn who is unaware that the party over there in the corner most probably has a bottle of brandy underneath the table and that the fat chap at the next table is most likely a foreigner, judging from the waiter's mystified look as he takes the order. And woe betide the newcomer if his tie is crooked or he has forgotten to make use of the clothes brush in the cloakroom. His self worth instantly plunges to several degrees below zero, something that can happen to the most respectable of men, unless he's an actor or in the company of a lady of dubious character. For, particularly in the latter case, prejudiced stares are likely to give way fast to a forgiving smile: well, well, at least that one's no stick-in-the-mud. He'll have something lined up for afterwards, you bet! Surpassing all expectations… Pity I have my young lady with me tonight, otherwise I'd try to tag along.

It was therefore somewhat of a relief for me to be going in accompanied by Ami, obediently following her confident march towards a table she was barely aware of yet, but which her inborn restaurant instinct had already scented out. Her father had been a billiards man and died when she was just a child. It would perhaps be going too far to say that her outward appearance placed her in the 'dubious' category, but there was enough substance to the allegation to ensure that we didn't meet with too critical a reception from the other diners. And I therefore felt proud of Ami as she proceeded in her unbothered and hence exhilarating way through the crossfire of undressing eyes, which, liking what they saw, swung in my direction with a: well, well, well, that's some catch you've made tonight, my man. Good on you!

Nevertheless we were still novices compared with the rest of the crowd as we sat down at the table and fleetingly absorbed those eternally important details that would help us merge with the rest of the crowd. To our right sat two gentlemen and a lady, busy drinking coffee, with the occasional sip at their glasses of beer. They raised these with a mixture of fear and pride and the democratic vessels clinked with surprise. To our left a solitary man modestly devoured a schnitzel, chewing with care and ceremony and every other second wiping his moustache with his napkin. A little farther away sat several young people: the girls flapping with barely suppressed envy as they contemplated Ami's coat, which I was helping her out of; the young men, students, barely able to contain their dejection as they compared Ami's attire with their own ladies' outfits. The head waiter was stationed by a table at the other end of the dance floor, endeavouring to resolve the age-old problem of all head waiters: how to play lackey and superior human being at one and the same time. In the left-hand corner, a group of people with flushed faces whisked their tea glasses under the table with virtuoso skill, and were then to be seen blissfully stirring the contents, which magically reached a third higher up the glass than before.

All this was taken in by Ami and me with roving, enquiring looks which snooped their nosy way around the room. And - once we had had our fill - we reclined, satisfied and content: we were no longer greenhorns, but old hands now and as blasé as the rest of them. And they were indeed beginning to view us with some understanding and sympathy, a sympathy which – given certain features of Ami's outward appearance – unmistakably grew and gradually promoted us to a category apart from the other guests. We had triumphed. We had been accepted as guests of honour in the restaurant's orthodox Ptolemaic world.

Ami's party was sitting some way off and could hardly see us, whereas we could observe them in the pillar-mounted mirror by our table. They did indeed look boring, I ascertained, not without a certain sense of gratification. I even experienced a desire to impart this to Ami, but could see she was too preoccupied studying the menu.

Although this was suddenly tossed aside.

– I want to dance.

But you just said you were tired, I objected in supreme untimely fashion. – Still, we haven't danced much lately, I added apologetically, for she had adjusted her clothes and taken to her feet: Come on!

–Taking to the dance floor in a restaurant is rarely a straightforward matter; on the contrary, you have to undergo a process of assimilation similar to that attending your initial entry into the room. For the dance floor is yet another world, strictly demarcated from that of the room by tables and chairs, though the rules awaiting novices are less puritanical. You may thus take liberties on the dance floor which would be forbidden beyond its borders and which, if the worst comes to the worst, you can always blame on the crush, or the slippery floor or whatever else comes to mind. It's strange, but you run less of a risk of making a fool of yourself on the floor than back at your table. For dancers are always watched by sitters with a certain envy, an envy that diminishes their capacity for criticism and lets them pass over such inherently deadly sins as two couples crashing into one another or the lady's shoe coming undone at the crucial moment.

But as I said earlier: the dance floor has its own laws, which demand absolute compliance from the very first step. Infringements are punished forthwith and as a matter of course; you lose the rhythm or tread on the lady's toes. Never mind that the crowd around you shows indulgence, the orchestra will strike up more ruthlessly than ever, inviting the saxophones to poke fun at you, making you long for the floor to swallow you up. The quintessence of these laws, – and this ought actually to be pinned to the walls of every dance establishment – is that while dancing your head should be empty of all thought or germ of a thought, i.e. you must try to put your brain into a state of temporary softening and absolute passivity. Speaking while dancing is therefore pretty much forbidden and, if you really must, for goodness sake don't say anything sensible, just converse in casual, illogical fashion, leaving your body free to go with the music.

These laws, in themselves straightforward and comprehensible to any normal human being, have one disadvantage, which you only discover on leaving the restaurant. Your brain, functioning like a piggybank into which impressions have been fed like coins throughout the evening, later refuses to process the stuff into a distinct representation of the evening's events; all you know is that you did or did not enjoy yourself, that the bill was such and such an amount, but apart from that you are none the wiser. The attempt to describe a restaurant scene – unless you build a purely schematic construct – thus confronts you with the selfsame difficulties you have when trying to retell dreams or explain imaginary representations: in both instances your brain is seriously unwilling to deliver up the material and you forever fall prey to the temptation to produce inventories of external happenings which, because of their mechanical nature, are of no value whatsoever in themselves.

Ami obeyed the laws of the dance floor with the reverence only original creators can have for their work. And she had taught me to abide by them unconditionally, at least when I was dancing with her. Yet it would be a big mistake to think that she danced particularly well or with true devotion. She always moved a bit too close, which sometimes embarrassed her and made her lose the rhythm. But she was incapable of doing otherwise. When we were out on the dance floor and she had laid her hand on my shoulder, her body pressed intuitively against mine and the pair of us, who over recent days had been so utterly shut off from one another, were in an instant so palpably close that all of a sudden I threw caution to the wind and started to talk to her properly – as we danced and the saxophones did their utmost to speed along the compulsory process of brain softening.

The consequences were not slow to follow. We crashed into one couple, bumped against another, and I saw Ami's head rear towards me from amidst the tangle of arms, backs and necks, bearing a look that clearly enough expressed a commanding: you just shut up! But I was by now high on this unexpected proximity to her and, helped along by a few glasses of brandy, which slowly permeated and saturated my whole body, I leant over her and said: I still haven't apologised for that... you know, that time. I really didn't mean to be hurtful, Ami darling. You don't have to say anything if you don't want to, but we can still be friends, can't we?

She nodded – actually a little too energetically for the movement to signal an answer – but since I could not see her face, only her curls as they fluttered and then settled back into the hairdresser's vision of waves, I took it as an answer, and we proceeded to bash into a chair which happened to have impinged on the dance floor.

This time Ami's head movement could not be misinterpreted. And we danced dumbly on, with her tightly pressed against me, something I pigheadedly insisted on viewing as connected with my words, filling me with a feeling of liberation and happiness, which I was astute enough not to articulate in words, but instead translated into quicker and longer steps. This made her cling even closer to me, whilst still keeping her head turned away, and when the music stopped and applause was heard around us, I too applauded with an enthusiasm that forced Ami to look up at me with surprise and then turn rapidly away with an ambiguous smile on her lips.

I cannot now grasp why I failed to notice anything at this point. Perhaps I was a little drunk. I certainly must have been so later on in the evening. For when we returned to our table, I in my crazily happy mood ordered glass after glass. We probably downed a whole bottle of brandy that night.

Back at the table I could speak freely. And I waxed lyrical over how happy I was now that everything was all right again and said how terribly sorry I was about my conduct and how I had spent the earlier part of that day running around the town waiting for it to be 6 o'clock and time to meet her. However I avoided speaking about what happened next, possibly because I myself could not properly explain our behaviour at that point, possibly also because it was a little too recent for me to dare to broach the matter in the same naïve and frank fashion as when talking about everything else.

She listened with a strange, semi-surprised, semi-distracted smile as she dreamily tapped her glass and looked past me into the body of the room. Occasionally she nodded and dutifully raised her glass to our resurrected friendship, upon which I resumed my speechifying. Henceforth we would meet every day; tomorrow we would have breakfast together, followed by an excursion to Ragnar Ström's place in the country. After all, it was ages since we had been there. I had run into him the other day and he had expressed surprise that we no longer appeared to want to visit him. Or – gosh, maybe we could motor out that evening, brandy in pocket – just like we did once before. How does that sound, Ami?

I must have been drunk that night. Although outwardly I seemed perfectly normal, apart from the fact that I just could not stop talking. For I would never otherwise have come out with such an idiotic suggestion. I ought to have known that in such situations Ami unquestionably had to be the one taking the initiative and mercilessly trounced any suggestion not emanating from her own brain. Therefore she said simply: It's raining this evening, and continued to look past me in the direction of a table somewhere at the opposite end of the restaurant.

But I kept on talking and raising my glass. And she listened with surprise, and then unwillingness, except I did not notice. Perhaps I did not want to notice. I did not want to let go of my illusion and used words to keep hold of it as long as possible. As long as I was talking about it, I could still believe in it. Had I stopped talking at that point, my illusion would perhaps have crumpled in an instant and I would never have enjoyed those blessed hours in a restaurant, a beer bottle of brandy before me and Ami's tired head distractedly nodding at my enthusiasm.

Presumably she had not the faintest idea where my elation came from. We had each entered the room in a foul mood, danced a few circuits and then had a couple of drinks. So how could she, Ami, possibly understand that, because she had clung tightly to me as we danced, I had drawn certain conclusions? Her practice was to press up against her escort, it is what she always did and she certainly did not stop to reflect on whether people might think it meant anything in particular. It was her way of dancing. She certainly felt just as distant from me as out in the foyer where we met. And that is why a surprised smile played on her lips as she looked past me and drummed distractedly on her glass.

By chance – I suppose I had dropped some matches on the floor and bent down to pick them up – I happened to look in the same direction as her. But all I could see was one head indifferently turning towards another head, which I could not see, but which was presumably visible from where Ami was sitting. I had already forgotten all about it as I offered her a light and ordered another drink, although it was already closing time and the bill already high enough.

Soon after, someone approached our table from that corner of the room. He took his time and I could tell from the sound of his step as he crossed the dance floor that it was the man with the grey hat. He came to a halt directly behind me, albeit a little to one side, and I saw Ami expectantly raise her head towards him.

I lit a cigarette and waited. Ami's eyes fastened on to him as he stood there behind me, but shifted away with a start as they remembered me and all at once darkened. The music struck up for the last time.

I bowed: May I? The man behind me in all probability did likewise. For Ami's eyes shot desperately back and forth between us and the light went out of them as, looking bewildered, she got up to go with him. But, since I likewise had got to my feet and moved nearer the dance floor, whilst he had to negotiate a table to get to her, she ended up going with me and all he got from her was a helpless, crestfallen look.

We danced, and I said not a word throughout. But then we

bumped into another couple again and Ami's head, which lay just as close to me as before, gave a jerk and thumped listlessly into my shoulder. And when we went back to our table, where an impressive bill awaited us, we were as distant from one another as we had been when we met in the foyer and spoke to our reflections in the mirror.

XII

The next day I was determined to see her, come what may. I had already made up my mind on this the previous day, as I lay in bed after walking her home along endless, empty streets, which put a final damper on any drive I had and deposited me in front of Ami's doorway, which - to the accompaniment of a reluctant: Goodnight, I enjoyed the evening - swallowed her up with a malicious clank. My brain, which during the walk home generated nothing but pressure on my forehead (relieved now and then by a snatch of some tune the orchestra had just been playing) exerted its strength in a desperate grimace before going utterly numb; and this in turn triggered a barmy, incontrovertible decision to meet up with Ami the following day – preferably first thing in the morning – and get an unequivocal answer out of her once and for all. Then I fell asleep before I had time to think the thought through; and when I awoke in the morning it still lay untouched in my consciousness, as categorical and ineffectual as 8 hours earlier. I started to fling on my clothes in order not to be late, and only after I had plunged my head into the washbasin and my brain half-heartedly and sluggishly began to stir did I begin to comprehend what had occurred the previous evening and to grasp that I was on my way to see Ami. But instead of deploying some practical sense or critical judgement, I stuck with the categorical approach since my initial clear-headedness had passed and was gradually giving way to a dull inability to process any material whatsoever: possibly the most defining symptom of a Finnish hangover. The seconds flowed past ever more slowly and once my ablutions were over I felt as though I'd already been up for hours and missed a host of opportunities to see Ami.

It was only 10 a.m. That meant she was still at home, I thought listlessly and sauntered over to the telephone on the desk. Three, maybe four steps were all that were required, but I recollect it took me an eternity to get there. It was as if time had been stretched, or virtually arrested, and I jumped more than once in the course of my approach to the table, startled by the fact that I had not yet arrived, even though my first step was so distant now that I could hardly remember it. And when Ami's voice, alien and remote, reached my ear, I was initially knocked off balance and mumbled something so rushed and meaningless that it took her a while to make sense of the situation. Then I heard myself talking into the receiver, faster and faster and more and more easily and Ami's voice filled in the gaps with her signature bland little laughs. Suddenly my voice started in horror and a second later I grasped the fact that Ami did not in the slightest share my yearning to meet up. She was going to be busy all day, the voice smiled blandly, and I could almost see her face before me, bleary-eyed and bored, but with a peculiar furrow across her brow, alluding to the night before and making perfectly clear there would be no repeat performance. – Maybe later on, she conceded after a pause, and if you put in an appearance at the café between 1 and 2, who knows, I might poke my head around the door. Mind you, I'm not promising anything, her intonation drummed home. This conversation is getting on my nerves and I'm anxious to bring it to an end. Bye for now; I heard a click from the receiver and bellowed a few hello, hellos down the line. Not that they ever reached their destination, for the click signalled that she had hung up her end; and she was now most likely stretching in her pyjamas like a sleek, coquettish cat, only to sink back into the divan pillows and have a jolly good yawn after this less than uplifting conversation.

But I was still far too bleary-eyed and drowsy to change tack with regard to our potential rendezvous and therefore clung to her promise of a possible meeting later on; I couldn't risk even the shadow of a doubt. There were just over 4 hours to go and I realized I literally had to kill them if I were to withstand their dreary, crawling pace. My hangover was increasingly making itself felt and it struck me that a glass of soda water could possibly help – and, what is more, would help pass the time; I'd have to put on my coat, go downstairs, walk out of the door, continue along the pavement until I reached the second crossroads, then turn into the Esplanade and on to the café. As much as 40 minutes would thereby be lopped off the time left to kill – that much was guaranteed – and afterwards I might hit on something else. I even began to worry there wouldn't be time enough for my expedition – for it stretched ahead in my imagination in the form of an endless, twisting path. Somewhere towards the end was the café; there I would be able to drink my soda water; and farther along was the point when I would see Ami. And, although this was still a fair way off, it was nonetheless very much closer than it had been a second or two ago when I rushed down the stairs with my overcoat unbuttoned, bringing myself closer to that final goal, now glimpsable and beckoning me on directly behind my immediate target: the café. I walked on fast; a chill wind snaked around the corner from the harbour, battered the brim of my hat and forced its way into my impassioned brain, blasting away the last scraps of thought. I found it refreshing and wanted to cry out, telling it to gust even harder; maybe I did yell something, but simultaneously barged into someone walking towards me and my fraught invocation to the wind shrivelled to a banal: I beg your pardon, my mistake. He eyed me crossly, I rushed on and reached the café foyer, hovering vacantly before an affronted mirror, which thrust my pallid countenance back at me: You had one too many last night, pal. I shrugged my shoulders and went on in, painfully aware that I would soon have to veer one way or the other and decide on a table. Luck had it that the aisle took me straight to one; I sat down, switched seat, realized that the new one was worse still and, my voice full of anxiety, ordered a bottle of Vichy water. The waitress looked at me benevolently, with a mixture of commiseration and envy; maybe she was in as much of a state as I was and could imagine nothing finer than to be leaning back in a chair and pressing her burning lips to a glass of soda water.

But she overestimated the relative privilege of my position;

the soda water tasted of smoke and encouraged a stifling dread to creep up my gullet. After just five minutes, all I wanted to do was get out of the room, which was distantly abuzz and visibly not best disposed towards me. A lady at a nearby table kept casting sideways glances at my bottle of soda water as she prattled on endlessly to her companion about the endless saga of her daughter, who had been having some sort of trouble at the office where she worked. A steady stream of words gushed forth; it was seemingly never-ending and pounded like lethally tedious grey rain against my eardrums. And, as she talked, time stretched into eternity, standing almost still – just as it had done earlier in the day when I rang Ami, except that I somehow experienced it more tangibly now. I no longer heard the meaning of the words emanating from the speaker's tireless vocal organ, only the letters, the pauses for breath, the emphases, which had no internal logic – endlessly accentuated and distended as they were, clogging the interminable minutes with their absurdly angular bodies.

I must have remained sitting there for an hour or so, engulfed in a maddening listlessness which tested my nerves to breaking point, since it was actually the product of a semi-lunatic expectation that Ami would any moment come in through the glass door opposite, a full three and a half hours earlier than promised (she always used to be at least twenty minutes late) – when lo, there she was, walking over to my table with a slightly affronted smile. I got clumsily to my feet, invited her to sit down, took a seat myself and was then at a complete loss. The window which had briefly opened for us yesterday was now well and truly shut; and the situation was evidently as distasteful to her as to me. She picked up the newspaper in which I had been aimlessly skimming the headlines and buried herself in it with a mere: Good morning, how are things? An awkward silence followed, heightened by the general hubbub and the tobacco smoke; and once again time stretched like an endless elastic band, which quivered at the slightest movement and sliced sharper into my nerves than before.

Eventually I hit upon a sentence which was capable, briefly at least, of breaking the bewitched circle in which we found ourselves. I said: How nice to get to see you – especially as you said earlier that you couldn't promise anything before 2. She raised her head, but without taking her eyes off the newspaper: Might you be waiting for someone else? If so, I can make a swift exit. But she gave no sign of putting her threat into action, instead remaining bent over the paper, a cup of now cold coffee in front of her. And after a short while she added: I won't be staying long in any case, I really don't feel up to much today. – And having slung the open newspaper over the chair next to her, she continued almost imploringly: I'm feeling so awfully tired today. Would you mind taking me home? I was astonished, taken aback by this sudden turnaround and gave an agreeably surprised, yet slightly sarcastic bow. With pleasure. Shall we leave right away?

She smiled vacantly in my direction. She appeared to be thinking something over, an activity that did not suit her one bit, for it made her face look 5 years older; and she already appeared more than her 22 years. I quite fancy going to the pictures tonight if I feel better by then. We haven't been to the pictures together for ages. We used to go such a lot.

Time contracted and no longer sliced so painfully into my nerves. I remembered a film Ami and I had seen in early spring the previous year. A sentimental American film, with Pola Negri's tired, worn face in a series of close-ups, and an undemanding, sentimental plot about a child robbed of its mother. At the time I had not yet learnt to appreciate the discreet principle governing American films, whereby they never dig too deep beneath the surface, but instead invite you to kill a couple of hours in the evening; which means that their content vanishes from your consciousness immediately afterwards – a principle no doubt just as acceptable as its opposite, embodied in German film, which generates nightmares or sadism. With the best will in the world I had been unable to share Ami's delight at the touching superficiality of it all and had given her a lesson in aesthetics – which she certainly tried to understand, for the unfamiliar phrases flattered her – although she frankly could not understand without ceasing to be herself. Superficiality was the only truth for her and she was not designed to go any deeper than the surface. It would nonetheless be unfair to portray this as a disadvantage; she was more directly attuned to the reality of the superficial than I was to life: this was patently obvious from her capacity to enter into it. I remember the touching, earnest look on her face as she listened to my lecture, proffering the occasional enthusiastic nod: of course, indeed, quite so. I could tell from the start that she understood not one iota, but the expression on her face so captivated me that I ploughed on with my (highly theoretical) attack on American film as we strolled down to the tram stop. And when the time came for her to climb aboard, and she reached out a hand to say goodbye, her face had taken on a solemn, serious look and she said: Next time we'll go to see a German film. Today's one really was a load of old rubbish. I was overcome by an irresistible urge either to laugh in her face or to embrace her right there in the middle of Studenthus Square. Except I could not make up my mind, at which juncture there was a clank and a shudder and the tram clattered off over the points, leaving me standing on the island where the stop was, despairing and delighting in the possession of a girl like Ami.

It is conceivable that she, too, remembered that evening, recalled possibly her thoughts and impressions as she sat in the tram after I had waved her goodbye, unable to follow since I remained standing on a traffic island at Studenthustorget whilst her tram slid away towards Tölö. For, seeing her sitting there right in front of me, forsaken – or possibly plain weary as she leant back in her seat – her face reflected something of the expression I had observed the other evening I was referring to; and that was possibly the reason why this indifferent, banal film all of a sudden came to life before my eyes. And, when we looked at one another, I at any rate had the feeling we had caught each other thinking the same thing; and a thin, timid smile slid over Ami's face, prompted by that memory which for a few moments smoothed away the wrinkles on her forehead – so particularly noticeable that morning.

– That really would be lovely, I replied, quite sincerely this time. Let's see – I reached for the newspaper – what films are on tonight. She leant earnestly over me, but then collapsed back into her seat, leaving behind something of the scent of her hair: silly me, it's Thursday; there is no film programme in today's paper.

I'll have a look when I get home, I said and she nodded: You do that, then ring me so that I know which picture house to go to. Although – once again a pained expression passed over her face – I honestly don't know if I'll be up to it.

Nonsense, you're simply suffering the after-effects of yesterday, I retorted cockily. For Ami's condition interested me not a whit, miserable and wretched as I was. And anyway it would be only natural for her to have a hangover.

XIII

I took Ami home by taxi. It was a saloon car and the air inside almost instantly became saturated with the scent of her hair. Not so much the actual perfume; there was something else, soporific and peculiar, like you sometimes get with wilting leaves. And, returning alone, I was swathed in a sense of languid repose, which melted into the soothing thought of seeing Ami again that evening and spending a few hours with her coat brushing against mine. I cannot claim that the prospect thrilled me exactly. I hadn't the least inclination to go to the pictures that day; I was more interested in what might happen afterwards: the stroll home, perhaps a little chat on her settee. To be honest, my perspective even on these eventualities was highly theoretical; I was far too tired and hungover to do much real embellishing apart from vague imaginings involving a vase of flowers on the little side table, with Ami clothed in a some kind of blue silk, which would stream over the settee and act as a cool antidote to my hammering head. There was very little eroticism in my representation and what tiny trace remained was solely calibrated to my need for something calming and aesthetic to provide succour for my sluggish brain; much as the person who has been on a long journey and arrives home dusty and weary desires mainly to take a bath before retiring, thus magnifying his enjoyment of the repose to come.

And, as sometimes happens when a seemingly quite unrelated occurrence triggers a train of thought or a mood, it was precisely that smell of wilting leaves flooding from Ami's hair and filling the sultry saloon on my journey home which, as I recall, soothed my breaking nerves and conjured up before my eyes an image so idyllic and placid that I suddenly felt content and happy and most certainly would have dropped off to sleep had the ride not been so short. Once home, I flung myself on the bed and spent the bulk of the day in a blissful and undeniably inane state from which I was only able to emerge and fumble my way to the telephone and reality when it was time to ring Ami and agree on a meeting place. She took an awfully long time to answer and what she said initially sounded so absurd that she had to say it over again for me eventually to grasp that she felt rotten, and could not come out, but instead wanted me to come to her and keep her company for a bit. – I'm so frightened– –, here her voice broke off and I heard the familiar click as she hung up the receiver, perhaps in order to enhance the effect and worry me, perhaps also because she was, as usual, simply speaking without thinking, without the slightest concern as to the impression words can create.

To start with I was merely annoyed about the fact that our sortie to the pictures – which now all of a sudden seemed to me of paramount importance – had been wiped from the programme with such flippancy and nonchalance. Not least because the idyll I had put together for afterwards now came tumbling down, i.e. acquired a number of realistic details which impinged on the general feel and threatened to turn the evening into a far from agreeable tête-à-tête with an individual who was either pretending to be, or actually was, sick. I therefore descended the stairs extremely slowly and grudgingly, bought a few flowers in a flower shop (making sure to select the cheapest) and rang her bell with all my might, thus giving vent to a portion of my exasperation and making it easier to produce the customary, well-mannered smile required on such occasions. She drew back the bolt and, as I was opening the door, I could hear her bare feet rapidly padding back into the room and falling silent as they reached the place where her bed stood. I clumsily removed my overcoat, somewhat taken aback by this reception, and when – goodness knows why – veritably bellowed hello into the darkened room where Ami in all probability was, she answered from somewhere far off (you'd have thought she'd pulled the blanket over her head or buried her face in the eiderdown) with a semi-muffled: come over here, please. I felt my way into the pitch darkness, banged into a table which had never before been in that position, but somewhere closer to the window, and eventually found the light switch. When the light flared up, I found myself standing next to Ami's bed, with her in it, turned towards me and fixing me with startled eyes that begged forgiveness.

This was another surprise. For a start, she had not combed her hair: the last thing anyone would have imagined her not doing. Secondly, she really did look ill. Thirdly – and this possibly surprised me most of all – the little round table which was normally in front of the settee had now been moved to her bedside, and – instead of the obligatory magazines - a glass of water and the empty wrapping of some medicinal powders lay there. This table, which I had knocked into when I entered the room, and which turned out not to be the table by the window as I had initially thought, instantly filled me with an uncomfortable sense that something serious might be in train, that it might not just have been a whim when Ami asked me to come over rather than go out to the pictures.

Her wide, scared eyes speeded up my internal metamorphosis, resulting in a bewildered feeling of tenderness and compassion, so strong as to vanquish in a second my innate discomfort in the presence of sick people. I sat down on the bed and leaned over her. The scent of her hair streamed in my direction, but it was a different scent from before, as if the leaves were now well and truly wilted; and I pulled away, startled, out of range. She groaned gently, took out her hand from under the cover and let it glide falteringly across until it eventually reached mine. I took it and experienced a damp, hot pressure. A good ten minutes was spent thus, with me staring at the glass of water on the table and feeling the pressure of her hand grow more and more uncomfortable and damp, and her curled up motionless under the blanket, which had stuck up in a sharp bump where her knees were.

The telephone delivered us from this situation in the end. It was a man's voice enquiring after Ami and when it was informed that she was in bed sick, it declared itself to be that of the head waiter. He had been told – he said – that Ami wasn't too well and was anxious therefore to hear how she was feeling. Was there anything he could do for her? It was somewhat awkward to organise things over the telephone and he was ringing from a telephone box, not from home, but perhaps he might pop his head around the door. – He didn't wish to bother her – heaven forbid – just to check what she might need and have it sent over from the restaurant. – I turned enquiringly towards Ami. The addition of a head waiter signified virtually unlimited supplies of brandy and it would therefore be foolish to decline his somewhat forward suggestion. She closed her eyes and nodded feebly. – Thank you very much indeed, I said into the receiver, we really appreciate your kind offer. Mademoiselle Ami may indeed wish to have a little something. We await your arrival. – I could just imagine his obsequious bow as he listened to those last words.

Another ten minutes passed, during which Ami endeavoured to explain to me what the matter was with her. Her temperature was clearly high, she had a sore throat and difficulty swallowing. A cold – we both thought – in which case it's a bit daft to have the head waiter round. But round he came. Barely had he reached the hallway than he was extracting from his pockets all kinds of mysterious packages which, once placed on the window ledge in Ami's room, offered the sumptuous spectacle of two bottles of brandy majestically towering over the circle of fruit and delicacies below.

The head waiter was short and portly and, in a few years, would doubtless be bald. He was in his element now, sitting himself right next to Ami's head, gently stroking her hand. And he proceeded with a single flourish to uncork one of the bottles whilst simultaneously spiriting forth some glasses – evidently from the restaurant. Time for a grog I think, he said turning again to Ami (who had noticeably livened up at the sight of the bottle) – if Mademoiselle has a sore throat, this will certainly help. Tomorrow morning I will send up coffee and a light breakfast, and after that I guarantee Mademoiselle will be perkier than ever. He leapt up from his chair and minced ceremoniously into the hall, where I heard him rustling around with some paper and, when he returned, he was if anything more assured and full of solemnity than before. He handed Ami the bunch of flowers with a deep bow – maybe there was just a trace of self-mockery there – which made her laugh out loud; she then managed a strained thank you, how very kind of you. I felt somehow left out during this episode, I was at a loss and therefore proposed we drink to something. Ami really did appear to have difficulty swallowing; she kept on coughing convulsively, but still asked for more. The head waiter whisked the bottle from between my fingers and poured her another glass, availing himself of the opportunity to have a good lean over her, whilst I remained planted behind his wide and worn tailcoat, growing increasingly irritated with the man.

He must have noticed this, for when we clinked glasses again, he rose to his feet and moved his chair aside to make room for me. I sat down on the edge of the bed and noticed that Ami's eyes had a drowsy look and were trying desperately to stay open; after which we clinked again and drank to her recovery. We then downed glass upon glass and Ami, who at the outset had valiantly tried to keep up, had a choking fit and somehow managed to curl up even more under the blanket. And for a long while she coughed desperately into the pillows, after which she turned towards the wall and closed her eyes. The head waiter's voice had dropped a few decibels to a velvety half-whisper, in which he recounted some of his ancient and oft-repeated stories, whilst we downed the remainder of the bottle. Ami was already asleep, and I wondered whether it wasn't about time the head waiter went. Yet the general ambiance had generated a great liking for the fellow on my part, a feeling which was beginning to upstage the entirely proper concern for Ami and her condition I had felt just half an hour before. It was a feeling which can perhaps best be visualized through a description of our mutual seating arrangements: the head waiter was sitting opposite me at the table, whereas Ami was behind me, so that I could not actually see her, but simply hear the occasional sound of her ragged breathing.

In the end the head waiter left. I followed him out into the hall and envied him in a way for having got himself off the hook so easily: he drank a couple of grogs and off he went, whereas I was now going to have to pay the price and possibly spend half the night sitting up with Ami. For something in her feverish, confused look told me to stay and be there for her, although I had not the foggiest idea how I could help. I once again sat down on the edge of the bed and she turned towards me with a sigh. Her tormented eyelids sagged over her burning face and all trace of that golden sheen was gone from her hair. The outline of her body was perceptible beneath the blanket, communicating a bewildered anxiety, which soon also had me in its grip and we looked at one another, fearful and enquiring, as if we intuitively knew what this anxiety meant, but were each trying to hide the fact from the other. Perhaps I did not adequately succeed, for Ami suddenly reared up from the pillows, the blanket slipped off her shoulders and her hands clung to me. I don't want – – you can't go yet – – I'm so frightened, she sobbed and her bare arms flung themselves around my neck, leaving me all of a sudden gasping for air. I carefully settled her back among the pillows, but her head resisted, thrusting upwards so as not to lose me from view, and her now thoroughly tousled locks swept despairingly over the pillowcase. I took her hand, carefully stroked her head and wondered if I should kiss her. I had not done so for ages and was afraid she might misinterpret things, or wonder whether I wasn't taking advantage of her condition, although heaven knows there was nothing attractive about her as she lay there in this state. But I still wanted to kiss her inasmuch as it might bring her some relief. My feelings were wholly genuine and this certainty should in a second have overridden any possible misgivings, had the origin of these not precisely been my consideration for her. And while I went on hesitating over whether or not to kiss her, I noticed she had dropped off to sleep; her hand had mine in a tight and damp grip from which I dared not withdraw, and I sat there for a long time, looking sometimes at the empty brandy bottle on the table, sometimes at her curls, which had now swept right across her face, leaving only a small bit of neck visible. The neck pulsated in a bid to fight off something which seemed to be tightening around it and the lobe of ear poking through, which normally bore a mother-of-pearl earring, had turned peony red with the strain of the battle being waged within its capillaries.

XIV

That was the last time I saw Ami. Several blustery days followed, with her in the hospital and me wandering around the city and buying flowers – which I handed to the nurse, for I was not allowed to visit in person. One morning I rang to ask how Ami was and the nurse's voice was shaking more than mine as we discussed what should be done with the body. It was an everyday, businesslike conversation, conducted from a telephone box at the railway station, and I seem to recollect having thanked her politely for the information. Then I set off down the Esplanade and was very cold. I felt no grief, in fact I felt nothing, just emptiness and the absence of warmth. A very cheerful acquaintance came up to me and I walked a little way with him, chatting and laughing along. But suddenly I heard him asking how Ami was and, when I answered, I understood from his face that she was dead. His expression had turned to one of such surprise and helplessness; his mouth wanted to continue laughing, whereas his sense of tact decreed condolences and sympathy, and I could not help feeling sorry for him. We walked silently to the end of the block, cleaving the solid stream of humanity flowing our way, then he swiftly turned into a side street and I continued on alone. The harbour opened up before me, the wind was howling, and I buttoned up my overcoat so as to feel less alone. The wind cut through my suit and shirt, tugged at them, and I listened to the sound of the cold, for it filled out the emptiness inside me and brought me somehow closer to reality. Someone wearing a coat like Ami's came towards me. She had Ami's fair hair and, spellbound, I tried to make out her face. But she was too far away and only when she had passed did I realize from her legs that she was a complete stranger whom I had taken

75

for a ghost, or rather who had inspired me with the crazy illusion that the last few days had been just a bad dream and I had, as several times before, happened to run into Ami while out walking.

In the afternoon I went to the restaurant. There was a tea dance and I sat down at a large table with a fine flower arrangement. I asked the waitress to take it away, but a few minutes later I felt so lonely that I moved to another table where a few acquaintances were drinking tea with rum. They attentively poured me a large one and, in the same way that the wind out at the harbour had filled up my loneliness, so the hot, scalding tea transformed it into solemn, deep pain. But that was fine by me, for it meant liberation from the rigid incomprehension that had had me in its grip all day, and the mood grew and expanded in time to the sentimental songs they were dancing to just a few steps from my table. These took on an entirely new meaning for me and I found myself softly humming along to the tunes, whilst a warm numbness filled my innermost being and was on the verge of drawing tears from my eyes. Embarrassed, I wiped them away, but the popular melodies drew forth more, and I sat there as if bewitched, feeling infinite relief and pain rise within me to the rhythm of the sound.

I took out my note book and began to write Ami a letter. I had done so every day while she was in hospital and it was really more out of habit that I did so now. I recall that I adopted a slightly teasing tone, but this collapsed after the first few sentences and the remainder turned into a desperate, banal cry to Ami for help, telling her only she could free me from the grey -cold loneliness in which I had been meandering aimlessly ever since the morning. And as I wrote, the now deserted room expanded, the walls pulled away from one another and threatened to slip into the void, whilst I shrank into a shivering ball of nerves, from which my hand protruded, letting the frenzied pen giddily dash across the paper.

XV

After that I was a hero for several weeks. People looked at me with guarded admiration, and I had nothing against that, for it helped me hide my hurt at Ami's death, and I am moreover a little susceptible to flattery and admiration. Overall things went pretty well. Occasionally I might of course happen to be in a café or restaurant and suddenly think I could see Ami in the mirror on the wall opposite, and once I was so shaken that I leapt up from my seat and sent my coffee cup flying across the table. But overall Ami left me in peace during the daytime, and it was only at night that I sometimes experienced a dreadful attack of jealousy vis-à-vis the man in the grey hat, who took on the form of one or other of my acquaintances, and if I then ran into the corresponding person in real life the following day, I had first to overcome my bitterness, which I generally hid by being exaggeratedly and showily jolly. One feature of the hero's role with which I had been saddled – and a dimension I possibly quite enjoyed – was that dozens of girls volunteered to take Ami's place, among them most of her friends and acquaintances. Quite possibly a moving and naïve attempt to offer consolation, but certainly involving a fair dose of veiled curiosity about the piquant situation that would follow. Who knows... But I was overly passive and lacking in initiative at this point, so I tended to say neither yes nor no, declining or accepting what these girls were friendly or silly enough to offer on a purely arbitrary basis. They could even on occasions be really good company, but their prying interest in the piquant side of things always led to the same result: they began to talk to me about Ami, normally praising her to the skies, and that sufficed to make me rise up like an angry beast. But my fear of loneliness meant that I inevitably ran into them again and I was grateful to them for being there – until an unthinking word had me fleeing to Ami's grave to clear away the ever thicker covering of autumn leaves and, transfixed, to stare at the wreathes with their now thoroughly faded ribbons. But I could not bear it for long there and was soon on my way back to the city, hungrier for human contact than ever before.

XVI

– Having come this far, the writer had to admit he was unsure where to go next. He stared for a while at Ami's photograph propped there in front of him, but its persistent habit of smiling inexorably at him led him to snatch it from its frame and find a replacement. Ami figured here too, but whereas the previous picture clearly dated from the period just before she died, this one showed young girl in a simple, short-sleeved dress. A certain coquettishness was arguably already discernible, but it was mitigated and held in check by the youthful vigour which seemed to flood forth from the photograph.

This particular one used to stand on Ami's dressing table and he would often contemplate it with a degree of curiosity, for it dated back to long before his first acquaintance with her. He had often pondered as to the nature of the live version of the picture and, when he had articulated this on one occasion, a shadow momentarily passed over Ami's face, although she quickly composed herself: you should have seen me then, I was a good little girl who did as Mummy and Daddy said and would never as much as spared you a glance. He could not quite establish at whom this particular side-swipe was aimed: it could as well have been a criticism of the writer himself, as a certain ironic melancholy at having been that good little girl 'who did as Mummy and Daddy said' and had not dared set free what underlay the coquettish pose in the picture. She liked to contemplate the image now and then, turning afterwards to the mirror for a comparison, and one could never predict the outcome of her scrutiny; sometimes she thought she looked better, younger, in the photograph, but if the writer idly happened to agree, she would sweep her powder puff across her face and spin challengingly in his direction: I see, you think I'm old and ugly, and her eyes flashed such that he ended up leaning forward to kiss her, to which she acquiesced after a flirtatious pause.

He had often asked her to let him have the picture, or at least let him borrow it to have copied, but she had always put him off, and only after her death had he simply gone and taken it. It stayed for a while on his desk, but then got put away, since he wanted her before him the way he had known her as he wrote this portrait. Yet now that the work was pretty much done and the picture had nothing more to tell, he noticed that that it still had not really yielded up all he had set out to portray. For Ami possessed certain features that were not visible in the photograph, features she generally neither sought, nor was able, to reveal, yet which could suddenly pop up at an unguarded moment and totally change the cast of her face.

This was most likely to happen when she made the acquaintance of someone who did not belong to her immediate circle and therefore in some sense represented something new and unexpected. There would be an initial few minutes during which she was liable to lose the poise he had so often admired in her, and something naïve and indescribably engaging would imprint itself on her face as her eyes felt their way inquisitively over the newcomer. The writer then tended to disengage from the situation, stayed in the wings and had little else to do but spectate. He tried not to appear jealous, smiled politely at everything, but all he got by way of reward were occasional distracted looks which, to his annoyance, settled and grew friendly as soon as they found their way back to the new person who, be it only for a few minutes, was now of interest to Ami. But as time went by he got used to all this and was able to enjoy such situations, especially as he knew for certain that her curiosity would soon be satisfied and her face would shortly regain that somewhat weary, serene expression which seemed to guarantee that she belonged to him. So he eventually learnt resignation and would sit on the sidelines and behave as if Ami were a complete stranger – who one knows will soon be gone, but who nonetheless exhibits something new and worth getting to the bottom of. He tended in such cases to screw up his eyes slightly when looking at her, for her familiar features were thereby blurred still further, and the fuzzy image landing on his retina gave his imagination free rein to complete the picture with things that were perhaps not there in reality. And then it occasionally happened that he forgot who it was sitting next to him, and from the nether recesses of his mind arose figures already forgotten, yet which suddenly came to life before his eyes, spirited forth by a vibration in Ami's voice or a lock of hair playing in novel fashion against her cheek. In such cases he could be relied upon to commit what in Ami's view was an unforgivable blunder, or more accurately a crime: he allowed his mind to wander and became an antisocial companion. For regardless of the fact that she took no further notice of him, little by little his aloof countenance unfailingly began to irritate her and she was quite capable of hurling herself at him in a bid to shake some life into the stiff and standoffish exterior he had shored against reality. He then duly experienced a sense of guilt and did his best to feel his way back to his fellow beings; but it never seemed to work. For whilst he had been absent, the others had already made some advances and he somehow felt left behind, unable to keep up with the conversation like the others, for to them what was currently being said fitted in with what had gone before and that he had missed. He grew ever more tense and after a few minutes of desperate exertion, which failed to generate anything stronger than a smile (intended as a sign of courtesy, but actually hapless and half-hearted) relapsed into his dozy state – until a furious look from Ami caused him to quiver back to life and sleepily survey the world around. During such episodes he could not avoid feeling jealous. It was a helpless, dispiriting jealousy which merely served to heighten his passivity, rendering it still more impenetrable. He did of course try to convince himself there were no grounds for his jealousy and that he, too, had received his share of inquisitive, interested looks from Ami at the time he had been a novelty for her. One might even say he had received advance payment, before even making her acquaintance. It had been a warm day at the end of April; he had been sitting at a table in some empty café and she was seated a few steps away by the window. The sunlight was streaming thickly and cloyingly over the room, which clearly felt embarrassed in the face of this critical and brazen prying. Ami, too, shaded her face from it and every so often shook her curls with vexation as she leafed through a magazine. He had remained sitting there, staring with sluggish curiosity at her profile and putting together his own story around her, as banal as it was improbable and impossible from any realistic point of view, with himself cast in the role of the noble hero. Initially he did it out of pure inertia; the newspaper he had opened and still held in his hands seemed manifestly inane in the thick light of the sun which streamed in through the windows in ever wider strips, but then a mood gradually developed which made the figments of his imagination come increasingly to life before his eyes, so he ended up pretty well convinced that any minute Ami would beckon him over to her table to keep her company. Next she would tell a long, sentimental story (which he would already know about) and beg him to help get her out of a tight corner only he could save her from. – At this point a discomforting thought raised its head: would he have enough money to pay her bill, for that tight corner from which he was to rescue her, despite all the romantic trimmings, somehow was linked to his making this grand gesture, which would immediately put him in a very different light in her eyes. He quickly reached into his pocket, the coins jingled and she lifted her head from her magazine and turned it towards him. He received a long, probing look and the beginnings of a smile, and realized that he had already been sitting there staring at her for some while. This discovery had the effect of a cold shower, waking him from his dreams at the very last minute, for he had already put aside the newspaper in order to get up and walk over to her, at which her weary smile was exchanged for a surprised look and a barely perceptible shrug of the shoulders.

He shamefacedly picked up the newspaper and sent a thick cloud of smoke in her direction; except it never reached its target, but collided with a pillar of sunlight and turned to dust.

She fidgeted, took out a mirror from her handbag, patted her hair a bit and then turned back towards him, as if to ask what he thought of the result. He must have expressed full satisfaction, for this time the smile actually materialized; it lingered on him and was then switched off by a clear act of will, for she energetically shrugged her shoulders and once more bent low over the magazine, so low that there could be no question of her actually reading it.

A dispiriting eternity followed, with him flapping around quite unnecessarily with the newspaper and her not daring to lift her head a centimetre higher. All kinds of visions whirled around in his brain, he experienced alternate waves of joy and disillusionment, but they eventually settled and he listened for signs of inner activity. It was as if the looks that had sparked between the pair of them had all of a sudden discharged their provision of energy – which had so far been a mere trickle filtering through the cumbersome fantasy creations holding him in their grip a few moments before; and the result was an emotional whirlwind far too potent not to peter out as fast as it came. He suddenly felt hurled back into reality and action was called for, if only to offset this fading inner energy. He rang for the waitress and paid. But as he was leaving the café, watching his step with infinite care, since he was sure Ami would see, he again sensed her stare burning into his back and hastily turned round, forgetting all the gravitas supposedly covering his retreat. This time they held one another's gaze, he probably even went so far as to give an enquiring twitch of the head – although she was set on not noticing. But the door instantly swallowed him up and he was standing in the entrance hall, somewhat lightheaded and quite unprepared to don his overcoat and face the street.

From that day forward the writer could see Ami coming.

XVII

It's quite conceivable that the picture the writer re-extracted from the drawer and placed on his desk was taken around the time he first set eyes on her. For when much later – it would have been at least a couple of years – he came to know her better and was in a position to study her directly, he sensed that the impression he had borne away from the stiflingly sunny café had nothing in common with the original apart from a certain portrait-like resemblance, less engaging however, since it stopped at her features and failed to capture her conduct or way of being. And there's no denying that the comparison was a little disillusioning, although he later observed an analogous process: over the period of their more intimate acquaintance, Ami changed still more and scarcely had anything in common with the illusory image that had imprinted itself on him on a certain occasion. It was as if this had faded or corroded in some way, although you might equally say that it had become considerably more concrete and less reality-resistant. Such a notion exasperated, yet energized him and, had it not been for the grey hat incident, maybe he would have succeeded in exposing Ami once and for all. At which point he would undoubtedly have tired of her and would scarcely have had any role to play when she died. Her ambivalent behaviour, however, invested her with something novel and enticing. And no sooner had they got to know one another a little better than he experienced a hollow sense of disillusionment, which nevertheless categorically spurred him on to the ensuing, gradual operation of undressing Ami. This was initiated in a more brutal fashion than subsequently proved advisable. The two of them got to know each other because, one stifling evening, they happened to land in a house with a party of near-strangers, who were unbelievably

84

boring and whiled away the time with an endless dinner. Record after record provided the accompaniment, with their host winding up the gramophone in feverish desperation, since he knew only too well that once the gramophone fell silent the party would unfailingly fall to pieces, leaving behind a gaping void which would be difficult to refill in a hurry. And this deadly ambience had somehow brought Ami and him closer than all the intimacies a day might conceivably accommodate could ever have done. They had barely exchanged a word in the course of the evening, but when they chanced upon one another in a shop a few days later they shook hands like old friends and surfed through the initial awkward minutes by recalling how deadly dull a time they had recently had in each other's company, thereby laying the foundation – as it were – for their very hastily established friendship. They walked out of the shop and launched forth together as if it were the most natural thing in the world and neither of them gave a thought to where they were actually going; they just kept on walking and the next thing they knew they were sitting on a bench in Brunnsparken, behaving precisely like all the other amorous couples around them. Ami had taken his walking stick in her hand and was poking around with it in the sand, whilst one of his arms gradually closed in on her waist, to which she acquiesced after an initial retreat to the most remote (and also most secluded) end of the bench. Their conversation had long since relinquished any independent meaning and he bombarded her with talk simply to see how she would react, for the play of her features afforded him a purely physical pleasure whilst she, shifting between surprise and seriousness, allowed her gaze to finger his exterior. At this point he slipped up somewhat, yielding to his unfortunate habit of observing people and things rather than cutting to the chase, and thus keeping up the repartee long after its mission had been accomplished – whilst Ami ever more impatiently poked around with his stick. She stared with fascination at the tips of his shoes and made so bold as to lean still closer in order to contemplate them more deeply, but he failed to notice anything until he uttered some platitude and discovered that it produced just as hearty a laugh as his earlier profundities. This discovery brought him down to earth and he at last took hold of her hand, which was fretfully moving to and fro in unsuccessful pursuit of a place to settle. From then on matters ran smoothly and, when he was on his way back after having walked her home and was nonchalantly replaying the events of the day, he already had a pretty clear picture of her in his mind; he knew she had a birthmark on the left side of her neck, her breasts were quite full and she possessed an intelligence and range of interests roughly matching those of most girls of her age – although she undoubtedly had some experience of the world and displayed an air of outer refinement. But even though this meant that the girl of his illusions was no more (or maybe it would be more correct to say: had a perfectly normal metabolism – she referred more than once on the way home to the supper that awaited her and which might, she feared, go cold) he nonetheless felt enough in love to envisage a rendezvous the following evening at the Kapellet café. And as he lay in bed, a plan had already taken shape in his brain, a fairly fantastical plan according to which he would likely have her the following day; certainly no later than the day after, at which point he would propose dinner at a restaurant, or even a motor car excursion to the country. He was far too sleepy to flesh out the next stage and far too sure of himself to bother his head about it. Why should he, with such a gratifying prospect just around the corner? On which note he fell asleep. But his psyche underwent some sort of metamorphosis as he dreamed; he saw Ami gliding towards him in a swathe of shimmering light, she homed in on him from all sides and an altogether new tenderness poured from her smile and into his heart. He awoke to the fiery sensation of being madly in love, brushed his teeth with celebratory fervour and cut himself several times as he shaved, at which point a towering question mark sprang threateningly out of the wardrobe: which suit should he don today? The choice was between a check summer outfit and a blue lounge suit, with a third option of light trousers and navy jacket. After prolonged and painful deliberation he decided upon the check, but then remembered its mortifying tendency to pull across the shoulders and put on the light trousers, whilst his brain was already working flat out on proposals for the most suitable tie. Ties, however, are not the most reliable of characters; the perfect bow can be in attendance six days in a row only to let you down on the seventh and then there is no option other than to grant the offender a little time off; after a few weeks its wayward behaviour will pass and it will become as slavishly obedient as you could wish a tie to be. The writer's tie line-up was in a particularly black mood that day and he was on the verge of giving up when a red and grey striped number finally condescended to form an acceptable kind of knot. He dared not put the jacket on yet and spent most of the morning in his shirtsleeves, for it was a bank holiday and he never had got the hang of how to derive benefit or pleasure from such occasions.

He therefore settled himself in an easy chair in the sitting room, hummed a snatch of a tune he had heard on the way back from seeing Ami home and gently smoothed out the creases in his trousers whenever they threatened trouble, given his incorrigible habit of sitting with his legs crossed. Inside him, like the memory of a good schnapps, glowed the fiery knowledge that he was in love and one ahead of the rest of humanity, ignorant as the latter was of the size and softness of Ami's eyes as she mounted the stairs and how delicious the movement of her arm had been as she waved goodbye. He was thoroughly content and quite unable to decide what to do. In the end he came up with what he thought was a brilliant idea: he would take a boat out to one of the small islands off the coast of the town and allow the sun to apply its rays to his new-born love, so that by evening it would be tempered and golden and ready for action. This decision unquestionably contained a dose of good sense, for nothing could be better for an amorous young man than a couple of hours at the local bathing spot. If he can manage to hold out against the dulling influence of the dazzling sun and retain an idealistic perspective on all the bare flesh proffered by womankind in bathing costumes, then his love is capable of moving mountains. If he fails, melancholy will be warded off by the general muzzy feeling that will inevitably hit him after having exposed front and back to the glare of the sun, so that his sole desire on arrival home is to eat himself into a stupor. A nice dip sobers a young man up and it can be no coincidence that the guardians of our morals turn a blind eye to the goings on at our bathing beaches, for they know that nothing works better against the temptation to commit foolhardy acts than contact with cold water.

He set off for a small island to the right of the town in a motor boat packed with office girls and shop assistants, and the vision of their billowing dresses took some of the shine off the more romantic side of things. The weather was heavenly and, once the boat had put in at the beach, he felt a bit heady and made off down a shady path, which echoed to the sound of shrieks and wails; for the bathing beach was just a few hundred yards away. Undressing in a beach hut, he was overcome by a fresh bout of mawkishness, for as he was carefully folding his trousers on the bench he began to associate the gloomy, stifling hut with Ami's stairwell, and his hand caressed the cloth, beige like a woman's skin, with something akin to tenderness. Next thing he was on the beach, standing tall so as to appear invincible and grand, for amidst all the noisy sparkling and splashing he had spied a girl in a dazzling, captivating bathing costume. She was sitting very near, frenetically burying her legs in the sand. Alongside her lay another girl, although he could not make out much of her at all, for she had virtually disappeared and all you could see was her sky-blue bathing cap poking up like a desultory flower minus its stalk. He decided that here was the place for a good fry in the sun, but first strode into the water so he could later observe the leg-burying with a clear conscience, as it promised to last a good while yet. It struck him how insufferably hot it was and he resolutely hurled himself into the maelstrom of waterily glistening arms and legs as they whipped up the sea into a confusion of seething and bubbling. The water appeared at a loss as it streamed tepidly amongst human bodies, and the waves strove in vain to restore order and cast back all uninvited guests on to the shore. The writer's mind was an absolute blank at this stage and, had he tried to gauge the temperature of his ardour, he

would resignedly have registered that it was approaching zero.
But he did eventually notice that he had been sitting long enough
in the water, which was now clammily cold and no longer
lukewarm as before and he remembered the girl burying her legs
in the sand. This conjured up visions of dryness and warmth, and
he resolutely picked his way back to the place where the sky-
blue giant flower was poking up like a buoy out of the sand.
Which was when he experienced his first disillusionment: by
now the other girl had seemingly expended her entire provision
of energy and no sooner had she caught sight of him than she
rushed like a madwoman into the water, where she lay on her
stomach and beat the water into a sand-coloured froth. This
image was a source of total mental confusion to him; it defied his
need for fine, warm grains of sand, and he resolutely turned his
heels towards her and pointed his head inland. Within a few
minutes he had sunk into a nirvana-like state of idiocy and
generalized reconciliation, from which he did not awake until
someone threw themselves down next to him with a snort. This
was immediately followed by the arrival of a number of drops of
water which stung his back and immediately evaporated, leaving
behind some hot grains of sand, which began to tickle, obliging
him to rise to his feet and shake them off. It was the leg-burying
girl, who had now hit upon a new occupation, wallowing in the
sand and groaning, not caring two hoots that her hair was avidly
attracting every grain of sand in the vicinity. The writer had
meanwhile been lying long enough in the glare of the sun to be
able to enjoy this cooling sight and therefore observed her
snaking movements with interest and satisfaction. He
endeavoured to familiarize himself with her bathing costume,
which was beginning to perturb him more and more: no easy
task, since its colourful splendour was still partly concealed by a
coat of wet sand. He did gradually manage though to get some
idea of her anatomy and face; she was fairly heavily built,
although when she was fully clad that would presumably not
have been so noticeable. Clearly this was her first outing of the
season at the beach, for she was not at all tanned and her wide,
large face was almost grey in its pallor and was undoubtedly

capable of donning a decidedly weary and unhappy look. But the pair of unusually – almost abnormally – wide-set eyes she would occasionally train on him, much to his embarrassment, lent the face a singular, not to say mysterious expression, and after a while he felt an irresistible urge to stride into the water and tame his growing agitation. He got up and had already put one foot in the water when the girl suddenly leapt up and charged past him, splashing him with sand and drops of water, so that for a few seconds he could see nothing whatsoever and had to wipe his face. Then he caught sight of her a few yards ahead, once again on her belly, hands and feet splashing, which prompted him to steer a careful ring around her before launching out to sea, safe from further attack.

They then lay for several hours alongside one another and he felt progressively more perturbed by her bathing costume and the piercing looks she gave him during pauses between her unusual gymnastic exercises, whether sand or water-based. Meanwhile the blue swimming cap remained dug in, motionless apart from regular hourly sorties into the sea, each lasting precisely 5 minutes, after which she returned to her spot. The situation was awkward, and he would have put an end to it long before – by introducing himself in some way, or quite simply leaving – had not his confounded romantico-analytical bent somehow compelled him to stay and, with the support of the few scraps of information available, piece together a picture of the girl's qualities and features. Starting up a conversation with her scared him, since he had already built up an image of her and did not fancy a repeat of the disillusionment he had experienced the previous evening with Ami. It is a lot pleasanter to be dealing with someone you don't know, if for no other reason than that you can behave much more recklessly in your head than in real life – and wary he certainly wasn't in his advances to the girl in the rainbow-coloured bathing costume (with which he had finally come to grips).

It should be noted in his defence that the possibility of her harbouring similar thoughts beneath her sand-filled curls can by no means be excluded. A reconstruction of their silent dialogue may well be of interest, although caution is advised, for we must not forget that the events were played out on a bathing beach in the dazzle of a hot sun. Not easy to put into literary form.

Still, with the appropriate degree of reworking, their dialogue ran as follows: (For understandable reasons, they used the familiar form of address and did not bother to answer one another's questions, although chance had it that a reply sometimes seemed to correspond). Him: why on earth did you buy that monstrosity of a bathing costume? Her: I'd like to know what kind of character you really are. Him: you don't seem to realize that a plain black one would make all the difference. Her: you could make yourself useful and buy me a glass of soda water. Him: could you please turn towards me a bit more, then I'll be able to see your breasts. Your position just now was perfect; yes, that's better. Her: you're welcome to look, but keep it to yourself. Him: you're quite wrong if you think I want to get to know you better, sweetie. It's too hot and things are much more relaxed the way we are. Her: you've got a mark on your neck where your collar button rubbed. Him: Ami's legs are more shapely than yours. Her: I get the feeling you're comparing me with someone... I'd love to know who you normally go around with.

Him: why are you staring like that? Is this how you always behave? Her: they say I look like Brigitte Helm. My friends even call me Brigitte. You can too if you wish. Him: if only you weren't wearing that bathing costume. Her: you've been looking down my cleavage for long enough now. And anyway, I want some sun on the other side too.

– As you can see, the conversation was all set to run its natural course; and had the writer not suddenly remembered that he needed to put his skates on if he wanted to get back to the town on time, a little naughtiness might have crept in. (Actually, it is conceivable that it already had, since the above is, as has been mentioned, a literary rendering.) He went back to the beach hut, and there a veritable metamorphosis took place; for when he emerged fully clothed, he was to all intents and purposes a normal human being. Ami had reclaimed her allotted place, except that a certain blending of widely divergent concepts had occurred. For his brain, softened as it was by effects of the blazing sun, was still too feeble to undertake a conscious eradication of Brigitte and replace her with Ami; it instead settled for slinging a dress over Brigitte's rainbow-coloured bathing costume and leaving it at that. The face with its eyes too wide apart stayed with him as he sat at the back of the motorboat and contemplated the vortex created by the propeller chasing along behind. And the face wasn't really dislodged until they reached the landing stage and a lorry suddenly loomed before the writer and nearly ran him over. It took the shock of this to bring him come back down to earth and give Ami her own form back, whilst Brigitte's bathing costume dissolved piece by piece in the dazzle of an ever-retreating sun and sank into the sea.

XVIII

Whilst he had allowed mood to dominate the previous day and totally thrown Ami with his many paradoxes, today he strode into action with icy calculation. As we have seen, the dazzle of the sun-soaked beach had been a bit too much for his infatuation, although the latter was elastic enough to have pretty much recuperated by 7 in the evening. The general course of events meant he was, shall we say, more soberly enamoured than before; the swim had washed away any dubious romanticism and, had not the writer felt a little sleepy, Ami would in all likelihood have spent that night in his bed. The fact is he had squeezed out of her what he fancied and then left her in the lurch, which was all the more unforgivable since he did so at a point when he knew for certain that she would have obeyed like a dog. It is unlikely that moral scruples came into play here; it was all about establishing his position as the one on top, although we shall soon see that he got this calculations badly wrong. He went home feeling rather pleased with himself, fell asleep immediately and spent the night on the bathing beach with Brigitte. The following day he ingenuously gave Ami a ring and was informed, in surprisingly chilly fashion, that she would not be free for two days. Despite his sleepiness, he had had to put a brake on himself when he abandoned her so arbitrarily the previous evening and retribution was now forthcoming in the shape of a vague jealousy, which put him out of sorts for the entire day. He sensed that things were apparently not as straightforward as he had imagined, that he had not in the least come to grips with Ami and that she had a private life which could yet deliver many a surprise. It is quite conceivable that his bizarre behaviour derived from that very intuition (which had already begun to surface) and ultimately he simply had not had the courage to play the game to its logical conclusion, since his vision of Ami would thereby have become far too finished and false and, most significantly, devoid of any future prospects. Before we get to know someone, our brain engages in an endless process of building up and knocking down, and the fact that our idea of that person ultimately stabilizes does not in the least mean that we have come to grips with their true essence; just that they simply no longer interest us. And had Ami been in a position to give him what he clearly wanted (for she had far too healthy a psyche to be capable of understanding this level of hair-splitting) his conception of her would probably have emerged fully rounded, which in turn would have led to lethal indifference on his part.

This danger had been overcome for the time being. He saw a flurry of unexpected opportunities opening up, amongst them a good many that were less than desirable. He therefore strode resolutely into action, mercilessly erased the impression of her he had been fostering until now and began to construct a new Ami, pacing up and down the room and feeling thoroughly fed up with both himself and the world at large. What was more, he had business worries. A full account of these would require at least 100 pages, so all we can do is gloss over them with the comment that they were no more serious than usual, which is by no means to say that they were minor. He handled them with daredevil recklessness and a good dash of energy; and by the end of the month he invariably fell prey to deep and genuine despair, which was nonetheless far too impetuous to last long. He would then relax with a feeling of having surmounted and survived a crisis – and ask for an advance on his salary, convinced he was a chap who really understood his business. On the day in question he suffered just such an attack of moral despair, which rapidly bamboozled his brain and prevented it from fully coming to grips with his new version of Ami. It is hard at the best of times to piece together a person in your mind after a deprecating phone conversation, and he sat down to put some kind of order into his finances, even if only on paper. He took a large sheet, drew columns on it and wrote down his outgoings and liabilities, producing an impressive list. As he worked, the income column meanwhile began inexorably to lag behind, rather like a genetically impaired child who, on top of everything else, has had to learn the tough lessons of life at a very tender age. He then lapsed into gloomy meditation, but refused to surrender and started lining up Income and Expenditure like two enemy armies. And, to his delight, he saw that Expenditure's numerically superior forces were nonetheless disorganized, whereas his fixed monthly salary had the firepower of a tank division, with cover from the long-range missiles of his potential literary earning capacity. He felt for a brief moment like a battlefield general, poised to rout a wild horde of barbarians; he could already see them retreating – until a bill of exchange, about to fall due any day, rallied the vacillating enemy troops into a counter-attack and the writer ended up having to draw down a two-month advance on his pay in order to boost his reserves in their fight against the furious onslaught of Debt. After which there was a generalized feeling of mutual flagging: Income and Expenditure faced one another indecisively and began digging themselves in. The writer was too weary to monitor the resulting war of attrition and locked the sheet of paper away in a drawer, all the while telling himself he had won a narrow victory. Then he remembered Ami, with a sinking premonition that she would be expensive, for even a child could see that she had her aspirations. He had a moment of hesitation and reached for the sheet of paper he had just put away, but was incapable of putting his decision into practice and collapsed into the chair, devoid of all willpower. This was perhaps the most fateful point in the progression of this tale; for in casting himself back into his chair with such abandon he had effectively ceded control over the course of events, and the story of his love for Ami became from then on a meaningless succession of coincidences and circumstances into which he was dragged as by the force of a current. And even the conscious and frankly megalomaniacal manner in which he sought to force her to her knees thus appeared to be the result of mere coincidence (as we have seen, it stemmed partly from something as prosaic as his growing sleepy after a bout of sunbathing) and, during his two days of waiting to see Ami, he ran the full gauntlet of a young man's humiliation through love.

By means of such an insignificant tactic, almost reflex, of covering her confusion with a chilly tone of voice, Ami had found his most tender spot, namely his tentativeness and indecision, both rooted in his eternal dilemma: whether to act or to remain a spectator. (The latter always had the greater appeal for him, but was for the time being out of the question.) And he confronted a similar problem now. He knew that the passive role he had been allotted for the coming two days would transform him into an astutely coolheaded observer of the meeting Ami had promised for Saturday afternoon, an observer who would be incapable of any semblance of action; and he understood all too well that action was precisely what was required here. This prospect gnawed at him and transformed any residual activity into ridiculous, meaningless gestures. He could sit for ages in front of the mirror, brooding over which features of his lean, ill-tempered visage would most likely impress Ami: an activity which usually ended, however, with his sticking out his tongue at his reflection, which immediately did likewise, and then turning away in horror to pick up a book, flick through it and, disgustedly toss it aside. Or he might be in the street and get the feeling he was being observed by a girl; in which case he'd adopt a Napoleonic demeanour and stare fiercely past her, whilst his inner self literally groaned with loneliness.

(This is where the writer's poetic nature perhaps comes through best: his inability to grasp people and situations as they really are, in and of themselves, without immediately trying to work them into some internally consistent design. Yet neither was he poet enough to be satisfied with the blueprints he assembled; instead he would end up fumbling his way gradually back to reality, which mercilessly smashed down his constructions. And that is precisely why this book is called 'To Pieces'.)

XIX

He took her a week or two later and felt his victory to be a matter
of pure coincidence, which it pretty much was: a mutual feeling
of oh-well-why-not, since both of them had realized they were
incapable of real love and therefore there was no point in
carrying on waiting for it. Whilst their initial encounters exuded
a refreshing whiff of improvisation, their meetings increasingly
came down to being bored in cafés, or on walks; and, thanks to
the inertia all this induced, Ami one evening allowed herself to
be led up to his room, where she obediently and indifferently
took off her clothes. He assisted throughout with stiff politeness,
which put a damper on any potential romanticism, but equally
saved the situation from unadulterated crudeness. For her clothes
had been off for a long time as far as his inner eye was concerned
and, as she removed her dress, all he experienced was the dry
sensation a scientist gets when, having elaborated a theory, he
finds its equivalence in the real world. She obediently left a few
hours later, he followed her out into the street and watched as her
silhouette was gradually erased by the dusk. But as he slowly
climbed the stairs, he was seized with a sense of having got
himself deeper in than usual this time, for something in her
demeanour as they said goodbye told him that this was by no
means the first and last time, and that she would certainly be
back. For they had discovered that they somehow suited one
another; neither was capable of deeper emotion, but each was
sensible and honest enough to acknowledge the fact. Both strove
in their respective ways to find reasons for satisfaction: he was
at liberty to probe her basically uncomplicated nature; she was
not alone vis-à-vis the rest of the world. This gradually generated
some kind of empathy between them – you might even call it

love, since the jealousy factor was one very important element – an empathy which drove them to seek each other out and spend a few dull hours together. The writer had always found Ami's company a bit dull as far back as he could remember. To be sure, one expedient the pair of them learnt to make assiduous use of was alcohol, which is why it has such a big role to play in this story. (No irreverence intended, nor any suggestion of impotence in their relationship; alcohol merely played much the same role for them as going to the pictures for other couples. The theory that lovers do this solely because it's dark inside is somewhat one-sided. Any sentiment needs to be nourished by a measure of novelty if it is not to wither into a habit.)

Another expedient was Ami's passion for motoring. She talked him into out-of-town jaunts, but always plonked herself next to the driver, leaving the writer on his own in the back, with a nice view of the meter mercilessly wringing Finnish Mark after Finnish Mark out of his wallet. Ami had a penchant for removing her hat, which sent her hair into a fluttering orbit, slapping against her face which, as the car gathered speed, lit up and was young again. Speed offered her an immediate and irresistible thrill, she succumbed totally to the pleasure of it and forgot all about him bobbing up and down on the back seat. They would normally alight at an open-air cafe, have a cup of coffee and take a walk. They were not good at enjoying nature, it was too alien to elicit in them anything other than purely aesthetic sentiments, and these in turn could lead to quite unforeseen sensations. For the sight of a clump of trees or a silted up pond deprived them of the certainties of the city and they felt lost and fearful amidst the disorganized tree trunks. In order to hide their disarray they lied to one another about how lovely it was to be away from the dusty streets and to tread upon soft, springy moss. And they said it so often that, on their return to the city, they almost believed it and one Sunday decided to arrange a whole day's outing. Luckily it was raining on the appointed day and the planned excursion preserved the appeal of an illusion and provided useful conversation material as he sat with a semi-recumbent Ami curled up beside him on the chaise longue, her extravagantly long cigarette-holder balanced between her lips.

But the conversation subsequently ground to a halt and the room was filled with a fragile silence which neither was inclined to disturb. She nestled closer to him, fearful of triggering the slightest sound, and laid her head upon his knees. Two frozen people endeavouring thus to melt the layer of ice separating them from the outside world. He tenderly stroked her hair and, since she did not move, quickly forgot about her. Not that he was engaged in thought, just letting certain ideas surface and subside unchallenged within the confines of his head. At one stage he saw Brigitte's face before him and his fingers learnt that her hair was as soft as Ami's. But when he bent over to kiss Brigitte in a sudden burst of passion, he encountered a surprised yet willing look from Ami and felt obliged to shoot into the hall and rescue his cigarettes from his overcoat pocket. At least that was how he explained his conduct to Ami; in reality, goodness knows why, his dash had taken him straight to the hall mirror and he all but flinched at the sight of the bewildered, half-crazed visage it cast back at him. From then on he kept a suspicious eye on Ami, as if to check that it really was her; and when they lay in bed and her head was just something vaguely outlined against the pillow, he suddenly leaned over and peered at her, causing her to sit up with a start and place a hand on his brow: you honestly shouldn't drink so much that you start seeing things. He laughed out loud, but at the same time saw Brigitte's wide-set eyes staring at him, and he buried his head in Ami's bosom, which she soothingly pressed against him as she gently murmured: it's all right, Ami's here. But a good while passed before he finally grew still; the clock on the bedside table ticked away in so reproving a fashion that he had a constant fight to call to mind something he knew was of paramount importance. And when he eventually did remember, he saw before him a dazzling, sun-soaked beach, with a swimsuited Brigitte burying her legs in the sand.

Epilogue

When the writer had completed this novel and received his fee, he made up his mind to drink it up. This was by no means some fanciful idea snatched from nowhere, but rather an imperative, which had accompanied him for several weeks and steadily grown more categorical. One Friday he withdrew the money from his account and divided it into two piles, the biggest of which he took with him when he went out that evening, determined to settle his account with the various individuals in this story.

These had been pursuing him day and night ever since he dropped off the manuscript at the publisher's, pushing themselves forward with the most unseemly claims and propositions. He had even heard rumour that Brigitte was planning to wed a commercial traveller, which utterly demolished the construction he had assembled of her. The critical verdict was that his tone was rather too gloomy, he had dwelled too much on insignificant details, had in places imitated Marcel Proust and been very hard on Ami. This last element in particular made him feel a little unsure of himself. Ami was dead, when all's said and done, and the dead can take revenge. Hadn't he turned her into too much of a type, one you find in novels and who lives on paper only?

These doubts propelled him along the streets of the small foreign town where he was temporarily living. It was autumn and a fine, stinging rain fell on the roofs, which looked lower and more unassuming than ever in the faint glow of the raindrops. He entered a small tavern, hidden in a courtyard, and downed a few glasses at the bar. The pressure he had been bearing eased for a moment, became anaesthetized, and he took several deep, long draughts before paying and taking his leave.

He hadn't the faintest idea where to go. The town boasted 6 taverns in all and he knew he'd end up doing the full round. But first he had to find himself some company (he was not overly fussy about which kind). For he was terrified all of a sudden of the reckoning yet to come that night and was keen to defer it. But the streets were scrubbed to a shine by the rain and pretty much devoid of people.

In the end he made a bee line for a restaurant where he knew that a barmaid, at the very least, would keep him company. It was a low-ceilinged, murky place, famed for its drunken bandleader: a fat, greasy Jew, whose suit always bore traces of beer and Zakuski. The writer sat down, ordered a bottle of brandy and found himself seated opposite a brightly painted Russian girl with an impressive appetite and who could drink like a trooper.

Half a bottle later, he discovered a certain similarity between her and Ami. The scrupulously puffed up peroxide coiffure and resignedly weary mouth were indeed remotely reminiscent of Ami with her fair, overwrought head. The new girl's name was Galya and the management of the restaurant paid her a dollar for every empty brandy bottle. She could get through 2½ on her own, she announced with professional pride and a strangely burlesque coquetry. Here's to us! He nodded distractedly, then anxiously scoured the room in search of possible acquaintances – for the barmaid gave him an unpleasant sense of slipperiness and cold. This was not a human being, but rather a container in human form, specially designed to hold so and so many litres.

She did thaw out after a while, however, and her features began to come to life, since the brandy had smudged away their rigid lines. She prattled and laughed in a cracked kind of voice, although the glint of a warmer timbre lurked, waiting to emerge from the depths which cagily shielded it from strangers' eyes. She leaned close and said: how about coming up to my room? I have a gramophone and we can dance. He recognized that same teasing, seductive look Ami put on when she wanted something badly, and he passively rose to his feet and followed her up the dark staircase leading to her room, which gave onto the same courtyard.

On the stairs she lost her footing, and softly and gently she subsided into his arms; her blind faith in his ability to catch her told him she was no longer entirely sober. He carried her up to a small and sparsely furnished room with an enormous gramophone horn glaring menacingly from a shelf in the corner. She sank on to the chaise longue and curled into a ball like a cat, whilst the writer nervously paced up and down the room and, anxious to find an outlet for his agitation, started up the gramophone. Meanwhile Galya had magically spirited forth a new bottle and two glasses. She also put on a robe of sorts, which barely held together across her bosom and afforded sight of an area of astonishingly delicate skin.

Time stretched onward in tedious melancholy.

Have you got a pen? he suddenly asked and took out his notebook.

She took this as an insult. A pen? What do you need a pen for?

There's something I need to write down before I forget – he said absently. Come on, can't you even get me a pen? he shrieked dementedly. Taken aback, she reached for her handbag and slung its contents across the table. A glass fell over. Here's a pen, damn it.

He perched next to her on the chaise longue and she leaned inquisitively over his shoulder. A strong whiff of face powder and brandy wafted his way and under its influence he scribbled down some hollow lines. What exactly was it he so urgently needed to write? He'd already forgotten, but a burning sense of whatever it was remained and his eyes helplessly scoured the room. Of course! He was to use some of Galya's traits to compete his portrait of Ami. But which ones? He struggled to keep pace with the movements of his pen, so tiny and flimsy all of a sudden that his fingers were unable to keep a proper grip.

Afterword
Per Stam

Translated by Dinah Cannell

Written between 1929 and 1930, Henry Parland's *To Pieces (on the developing of Velox paper)* is a short, unfinished – and very European – novel. Its author was, by circumstance, a cosmopolitan. His family (of German-Baltic and English origins) lived in Finland. He wrote in Swedish, which was his fourth language. And he composed his posthumously published novel in father-imposed exile in Lithuania, where he died.

The novel's subject is its own genesis. Or, more specifically: how to remember and describe things in a manner that chimes with reality. The narrator, Henry, has had a relationship with Ami. She is now dead. He is adamant that he never loved her (although he does miss her). His memories are difficult to capture; he is sceptical of their literary potency and wonders about their value as truths. His painstakingly constructed images of Ami are constantly exposed as incomplete: doomed to fall to pieces. Hence the title of the novel.

To Pieces was first published in 1932 and has since appeared in various versions. The latest of these is my own critical edition, published in 2005, which serves as the basis for Dinah Cannell's translation. Parland's text is a beacon of modernist novel-writing in Swedish. It stands as a minor classic of Swedish and Finland-Swedish literature and is constantly attracting new readers. There are now translations available in all the languages Parland either already mastered or was in the process of acquiring: German, Russian, Finnish, French and Lithuanian.

Henry Parland (1908–1930) was born in Vyborg, part of the Grand Duchy of Finland at that time. His parents had English and German-Baltic roots and his early years were spent in Russia. After the Revolution, as the 1920s approached, they settled in the newly independent Finnish state. Henry, the eldest of four brothers, went to the Swedish school in Grankulla on the outskirts of Helsinki. In the wake of German, Russian and Finnish, Swedish became his fourth language and the one in which he would write. Although it enjoys official status, Swedish is a minority language in Finland, spoken as mother tongue at the start of the twentieth century by around 10% of the population.

After he had completed his school leaving certificate in 1927, Parland spent two years 'studying law' at Helsinki University. In reality, he attended the 'university of life' and served his writer's apprenticeship. Life became literature and literature the purpose of life. He collaborated on the newly founded *Quosego. Tidskrift för ny generation* (1928-29) (Quosego: Journal for a New Generation). Fellow authors included Elmar Diktonius, Hagar Olsson, Gunnar Björling and Rabbe Enckell – somewhat more established figures within the world of modernist poetry. Finland-Swedish Expressionism (Parland's term) had been termed 'modernist' as a gesture of scorn, but the new group were able to reverse this negative charge. Fifteen years before the breakthrough of modernism in Sweden, Finland-Swedish modernists like Edith Södergran and Hagar Olsson were stirring up the literary landscape. *Poems* by Södergran (1892–1923) appeared as early as 1916 and Diktonius, Björling and Enckell were publishing their first work by the beginning of the 1920s. Poetic renewal was at the heart of their joint enterprise: free verse, bold images, everyday language and – in some cases – downright provocation. Henry Parland was full of admiration for Södergran, who died young. He was equally drawn to the work of Diktonius and Björling and was to find himself admitted as one of their circle, where he gained notoriety as the youngest member of that first generation of Finland-Swedish modernist writers.

Henry Parland knew from the outset what he wanted. He had tried, and failed, to publish a poetry collection as early as 1927. A year or so later, however, things looked up and *Idealrealisation* came out in the spring of 1929. A carefully selected and consciously crafted volume, it stands as a brilliant example of twentieth-century Finland-Swedish lyric writing. (A parallel-text English translation by Johannes Göransson, entitled *Ideals Clearance*, was published by Ugly Duckling Presse, Brooklyn in 2007.) The book is divided into four sections: 'Stains', 'Socks', 'Flu' and 'Grimaces'. The title and subheadings are taken from individual poems in the collection.

> The Clearance Sale of Ideals
> – You say it has already begun.
> But I say:
> Better cut the prices.
>   ('Socks' VI.)

The poems are written in a highly concentrated style. An airy lightness characterizes them and they are designedly rough at the edges. Readers are addressed directly, their attention seized through exclamations, questions, colloquialisms. The poetic 'I' moves confidently within the world it has created. Parland's verse is not emotionally cold; it is distanced.

> That's not me.
> That's a mouth exhaling smoke,
> eyes that have seen too many people,
> a brain jazzing wearily.
>   ('Flu' VIII.)

Parland often uses the literary device of 'animation': endowing inanimate objects with a life of their own. Indeed, one of his *Quosego* texts was aptly entitled 'The Revolt of Things'.

It was only a matter of time before Parland's not-quite-so-straightforward existence was exposed: neglected studies, skating on the back of risky IOUs, heavy drinking and a messy love life. Socially demeaned by the Revolution, his parents had invested many a hope in their gifted eldest son – who failed to deliver. Not yet twenty-one, with *Ideals Clearance* barely back from the printers, he was dispatched to Kaunas in Lithuania in May 1929, where his maternal uncle Vilhelm Sesemann (1884–

1963) was then living. Sesemann had left Soviet Russia a few years after the Revolution, taking up a professorship in philosophy at Kaunas University in 1923. His family settled in Paris, however.

Henry Parland's parents wanted him to have a new start; and, to some extent, that is what he got. He was offered a part-time secretarial position at the Swedish consulate. He studied French and read Gide and Proust; he wrote articles for Lithuanian and Finland-Swedish newspapers and periodicals; he became acquainted with Lithuanian writers and journalists. Yet his letters home speak also of loneliness and the feeling of being an outsider. Drink played its part, too. During the summer of 1929, some of his poems appeared in Lithuanian translation in the journal *Naujas Žodis* (The New Word). Articles in German, mainly on Finnish and Nordic literature, featured in various Lithuanian publications: *Vairas* (The Helm – the National Party's official organ), the academic periodical *Židynis* (The Hearth), the revolutionary *Trečias Frontas* (The Third Front) and *Naujas Žodis*.

He also reported on his Lithuanian experiences for the Finland-Swedish press, in particular the Swedish language daily *Hufvudstadsbladet*. Among other things, he covered the activities of the Jewish theatre studio, Soviet cinema (banned in Finland) and the grave of the unknown soldier. He produced a piece entitled 'The Modernist Poem: a Formalist Perspective', introducing Nordic readers to the theory of Russian Formalism. The fifth issue of *Quosego*, in which the article was to appear, never materialized and publication took place posthumously.

Thanks to the range, understanding and originality of his cultural journalism, Henry Parland has subsequently been described – with fitting exaggeration – as a kind of Roland Barthes *avant la lettre* (Eero Tarasti, 1990).

Parland wrote *To Pieces* in Kaunas between November 1929 and August/September 1930. He had intended to enter the novel for a pan-Nordic prize. 'Scandinavian literature currently appears to be madly in search of the novel', he argued in his articles on the younger generation of Scandinavian writers. He saw the

competition for best Nordic novel as an attempt to polish the
fading image of Swedish literature. (The prize money was
'dizzying,' he wrote.) With the exception of Hagar Olsson, the
Finland-Swedish modernists had not really explored the novel as
an art form. Even Olsson confined her progressiveness to content
rather than novelistic form. Other members of the group – prizes
or otherwise – began to venture in the direction of the novel
around 1930. Enckell produced a series of quiet, intimate prose
texts; Diktonius wrote *Janne Kubik. Ett träsnitt i ord* (1932)
(Janne Kubik: a Woodcut in Words); and rumour has it that
Björling himself tried his hand, working on a novel called Gurka
– now untraceable. Be that as it may, Parland and Diktonius were
the most radical experimenters and theirs are the novels to have
stood the test of time.

The germ of *To Pieces* lay dormant all along. Parland himself
arguably provided the best account of its origins in a letter from
1930:

> My main concern at the moment is my novel. It has
> given new substance to my existence and I haven't
> once been in a bad mood all week. This has never
> happened to me before. And the novel is walking on
> its own two legs. (…) My story has a touch of Proust
> – whose stimulating effect on me I have possibly
> written to you about before. The subject matter is
> interwoven with the operation of memory within me
> as I write: a process which in turn engenders the
> book. The whole thing starts with developing
> photographs. The memories then emerge and spread
> over page after page.
> (Letter to his mother, Maria Parland, 8 February,
> 1930.)

The manuscript has a beginning, middle and end, but was
never finally revised. Its author had various ideas as to how to
rework the text, but they never came to fruition.

Henry Parland died of scarlet fever in November 1930 at the

age of 22. He had been due to start work a few weeks later at the new Lithuanian branch of Ivar Kreuger's Swedish Match. He was buried in Kaunas.

*

> The whole joy of a photograph lies in those previously unobserved details; once you are used to them and your image of the subject in question is complete, the picture itself is of no further interest. A photograph thus turns out to have a very short lifespan. After just a few hours it appears rather forlorn and bygone and is best put aside and forgotten – until one day, by chance, you are visited by that same sense of immediacy and novelty that comes when small and trivial details make the remembrance of something quite removed and forgotten flash up with all the compelling brightness and suggestive illusion of reality. Never do you get a stronger sense of this than when you are bent over a developing bath and feature after feature shoots forth, each one complementing – giving new meaning and weight to – the next and finally coalescing as a picture which, wide-eyed, takes in the room like a newborn child.
>
> (From *To Pieces*, Chapter II.)

The novel *To Pieces (on the developing of Velox paper)* is very contemporary in feel. There are detailed descriptions of the workings of a Zeiss Ikon camera and of the various fluids and types of paper required to develop a photograph. There is discussion of the merits of American versus German film. The reader learns about Finnish café life under Prohibition and how to double-cross the alcohol ban. Dance floor etiquette is broached, as are the rules for flirting on the beach. Yet Parland simultaneously breaks through the boundaries of contemporary writing. We are not offered standard textbook prose in the descriptive passages on photography; the actual taking of photographs functions as a metaphor for the way memory works. In one of the most intricate sections of the book, the operation of the subconscious is portrayed through allusion to the act of memory, the process of photography and – fishing (Chapter IX).

Drawing on a mix of contemporary modernist writing – from Russian futurism, Finland-Swedish modernism, to the work of contemporary French novelists – Henry Parland produced something very much his own. As mentioned earlier, his enquiries into the workings of memory were influenced by Marcel Proust's *In Search of Lost Time* (*À la recherche du temps perdu*), in particular the depiction of the Swann-Odette and the Marcel-Albertine relationships. Swann and Marcel would seem to have melded into the narrator Henry, while Henry's Ami carries with her the stuff of her literary predecessors Odette and Albertine. With an ironic wink, Parland acknowledges his Proustian kinship by prefacing the text proper with a short motto: 'This book is perhaps a plagiarism of Marcel Proust'; and further allusions are to be found in the Epilogue. In terms of narrative technique, the two writers clearly share similarities. Unlike Proust, however, Parland works with consciously evoked memories, using photographs of Ami and an encounter with a grey hat to trigger the recollection process.

The novel is also inspired by the Russian literary theory known as formalism. In Kaunas, Parland read Viktor Shklovsky. From a theoretical point of view, Shklovsky's most significant concepts were 'automization' and 'estrangement'. The idea was to foreground the process of perception itself, thereby rendering the familiar strange and enabling people to rediscover their lost sensibility. 'Make it new', wrote Ezra Pound. Henry Parland expressed the idea as follows in his essay on the modernist poem from a formalist perspective:

> – We live our daily lives with a clear line of demarcation between ourselves and the rest of the world. We perceive things around us, but feel no connection with them; they leave us indifferent. We are so used to seeing them in their usual places that

we do not notice them.
The task of the poem is to give us back a living link
with our surroundings. To do this it must wrest things
from their everyday context and put them in a new
and striking setting. Our sense of novelty and
immediacy triggers a mental reaction, i.e. a poetic
experience

To begin with, the reader of *To Pieces* is informed that
shaving mirrors and cameras crave new impressions if they are
not to grow tired; and that a photograph can only provide a
'sense of immediacy and novelty' under special circumstances.
Initially, memories of Ami come to Henry while he is developing
a photograph: he sees details he had not noticed before. Even the
relationship between Ami and Henry is described and played out
in terms of automization and estrangement. The love story is put
together in a matter of fact way, without flourishes and
sentimentality. This does not necessarily deliver clarity, but we
are left wondering, scratching our heads in a bid to solve the
riddle.

To Pieces is also the work of a writer coming to grips with
real-life tragedy: a literary settling of personal accounts. Yet the
novel also seems to be holding something back. What is it about
Ami that has to be kept quiet – or cannot be spoken? Why is it
that Henry does not tell it as it is with regard to the relationship?
He never quite manages to describe Ami to his satisfaction and
the novel closes with a doomed attempt to provide the finishing
touches to her portrait. Maybe the whole novel is ultimately a
circling-around: an attempt to get as close as possible to the goal
without being consumed by fire.

To Pieces is a vibrant and multi-layered work. Every reader
will have his or her way of apprehending it. One may be drawn
by any number of things: the playfulness of the writing; the
author's manifest glee in narration; his wry descriptions of
Henry wrestling with his world and his memories; the underlying
darkness; and the unspoken dimension of the Henry-Ami story.

People should read the book, however, not because it is an

icon of Swedish modernism or because the literary critics love it. They should read it because it is living literature: funny, clever – and touched by pain.

*

To Pieces was published posthumously in 1932 in the volume *Återsken* (Reflections). Gunnar Björling and Rabbe Enckell took main editorial responsibility for this collection, which also comprised poems, short stories and articles. The twenty chapters from the manuscript of just over 120 pages were reproduced in their rightful order. It was Parland's linguistic style that caused some headaches: occasionally his prose was negatively coloured by influences from other languages. The editors opted for full alignment with contemporary Swedish norms. This meant getting rid of 'Finlandisms', where Finland-Swedish deviated from standard Swedish, and weeding out German-influenced turns of phrase. There was some deletion and, in order to protect privacy, characters who might be recognised had their names changed. (The narrator, Parland, was renamed Rapp, for example.) The underlying purpose appears to have been to discourage people from reading the text as a *roman-à-clef* and to deal – via deletion or editing – with sections of the text deemed less than literary. Björling, that most linguistically radical of the modernists, ironically emerges as the most fervent 'improver'.

In the 1960s, Henry Parland's brother Oscar published a three-volume edition of his older sibling's work. This contained poems, prose, and criticism. A new version of *To Pieces* then came out in 1966 as part of *Den stora Dagenefter. Samlad prosa 1* (The Great Morning After: Collected Prose I). Most of the names and deleted passages were restored in this second edition, but the linguistic alignment of the 1930s remained and Parland's language was brought up to date. The main distinguishing factor between the two editions, however, is the use of material from notebooks and sources other than the main manuscript. An attempt was made to deliver and expand on what the author had himself planned by way of revision. As a result, changes were made to the sequence of chapters and the novel was divided into three parts, rather than two.

This second edition was the basis for the first solo publication of *To Pieces* in 1987, culminating in further linguistic alignment and the removal of any remaining 'Finlandisms'.

By the turn of the millennium, following all this major and minor reworking, the novel had moved more and more away from Henry Parland's original. *To Pieces* was now an artwork in need of restoration. The 2005 critical edition grew out of my doctoral thesis (Per Stam, *Krapula. Henry Parland och romanprojektet Sönder*, 1998) and was based on the original manuscript. I kept alterations and alignments to a minimum. Apart from a few instances where corrections were deemed necessary, pencil amendments by the various editors were rejected. Parland's sequence of chapters in the main manuscript was reinstated and the text was again divided into two parts, preceded by an introductory chapter or prologue, plus an epilogue. As to the additional sections and passages on which the author was working during the summer and autumn of 1930, only five paragraphs were incorporated into the main manuscript. They now constitute the end of the Epilogue. ('Time stretched away into long-drawn out melancholy ...' etc.)

Every effort was made to preserve Henry Parland's particular style: the Finland-Swedish words and expressions; the everyday language; use of slang; peculiar coinages, be they conscious or unconscious; unusual sentence structure. Equally respected was his atypical use of dashes, as well as his unconventional punctuation. The manuscript is a glossary in its own right of 'Finlandisms' and a text-book illustration the kind of mistakes that anyone learning Swedish as a foreign language is likely to make. An anachronistic way of describing *To Pieces* would be to say that it is a modernist classic written in immigrant Swedish; or, better still, immigrant Finland-Swedish. It is not unusual, moreover, for authors to write in languages that are relatively new and unfamiliar. Conrad and Beckett did; and even Strindberg occasionally composed in French.

The new critical edition of *To Pieces* was well received in both Finland and Sweden. The liberal editorial approach appears to have paid off, since modern readers clearly relished Parland's special way with language and had no problem relating to the text. 'Parland's status as a linguistic outsider lends the novel its peculiar vitality and ease of expression', wrote Carl-Johan Malmberg in the Swedish broadsheet *Svenska Dagbladet* (25 September, 2005). He then went on to say:

> It is also a book about the loneliness of being young. The reader is fed a raw testimony in the garb of sophisticated experimental prose. There is more than clever artistry at work: the writer's openly declared struggle to find an appropriate form for his novel is not just literary bravado. His estrangement from literary conventions – and from language itself – mirrors the estrangement he feels in life.
>
> When everything is seen through an illusion, how is one to achieve poise in love and life? As an embodiment of the search for a way to live in the workaday world, *To Pieces* is quite simply in a league of its own.
>
> (– – –)
>
> Gunnar Björling once described Henry Parland as 'a light illuminating the loony bin of life'. *To Pieces* may not be readily understood, but leaves one with greater understanding. It is a book that screams intelligence.

Other critics have drawn particular attention to the language of the novel and the unusual starting point of the author. 'A sense of exile born of a life in a linguistic melting pot: not Finnish, yet Finnish; Swedish, yet not Swedish; not Russian, yet abutting Russia and its onward-moving futurism and formalism. And, at the heart of it all: a 'nothing', a vacuum, which proves to be a bottomless source for Henry Parland's frantic ladle.' So said Joar Tilberg in the Sweden's tabloid *Aftonbladet* (31 August, 2005). Tiberg deems it deprecating to endow *To Pieces* with cult status, for the novel endures 'as an undercurrent' beneath the literary production of the decades following its production. 'Ruptured chronology, hyper-sensitive attention to detail, branching composition, a sense of the absurd, the novel as a launch into the blue... profoundly claustrophobic and ambivalent in terms of content and style.'

There are also strong words of praise in Jonas Thente's summary of the literary output from 2005 in Sweden's *Dagens Nyheter* (December 13, 2005):

> A masterpiece that fate dictated should stay unfinished. A Nordic novel – the only one I know – that is thoroughly modern. Neither before nor after has a writer succeeded in making a Nordic city the locus of a Zeitgeist. Yet that is precisely what Helsinki is in Parland's stylish, fractured, guarded novel. Vladimir Mayakovsky, Hjalmar Söderberg and Boris Vian would have been envious. Per Stam's critical edition is simply superb.

This edition of the novel has been translated into French, German, Russian, English and Lithuanian. The translations were well received in their respective countries. *Frankfurter Allgemeine Zeitung*, serialized the novel as *Zerbrochen* in the autumn of 2007. 'Readers will discover a small masterpiece, rich in subtlety and perception: a true modernist classic, which wistfully draws the gaze towards new horizons.' This was the verdict of the paper's reviewer, Richard Kämmerling ('Das Zittern der Zeit' ('Time doth tremble'), 27 September, 2007). By 1 January 2008, Zerbrochen shared fourth place in the German critics' Top Ten.

So perhaps Henry Parland is, at last, about to conquer Europe.

> Good Lord,
> let's rather
> write poetry in money
> like Ivar Kreuger

or Basil Saharoff;
they don't give a damn about the Nobel Prize.
Tear a sheet out of history
and write a receipt.
Received Europe
which is hereby acknowledged.

(Translated by Johannes Göransson and reprinted by permission.)

Literature

1. About Henry Parland

Oscar Parland, *Kunskap och inlevelse. Essayer och minnen* (Knowledge and Feeling: Essays and Memories), Helsinki: Schildts 1991.

Oscar Parland, "Gunnar Björling och Henry Parland", Clas Zilliacus & Michel Ekman (red.), *Björlingstudier. Föredrag vid Gunnar Björling-symposiet den 18–19 maj 1992*, Helsinki: Svenska litteratursällskapet i Finland 1993, pp. 31–54.

Karin Petherick, "Four Finland-Swedish Prose Modernists: Aspects of the Work of Hagar Olsson, Henry Parland, Elmer Diktonius and Rabbe Enckell", *Scandinavica. An International Journal of Scandinavian Studies*, Special issue devoted to Modernism in Finland-Swedish Literature, 1976, pp. 45–62.

Jana Prikryl, "Photo Finnish. The snapshot poems of Henry Parland", Poetry Foundation, 2009. (www.poetryfoundation.org/ journal/article.html?id=181477, 24 January 2011).

Agneta Rahikainen (red.), *Jag är ju utlänning vart jag än kommer. En bok om Henry Parland*, Helsinki: Svenska litteratursällskapet i Finland/Stockholm: Atlantis 2009.

Per Stam, "Henry Parland in Lithuania", Vilnius. *Lithuanian Literature Culture History Winter 1996* (Magazine of the Lithuanian Writer's Union), pp. 112–131. (Also in Lithuanian, "Henri Parlandis Lietuvoje", *Metai: Literatura, Kritika, Eseistika* 10: 1998, pp. 123–137.)

Per Stam, "'Motto: denna bok är kanske ett plagiat av Marcel Proust' – Henry Parland och Marcel Proust", Maria Hjorth & Ingrid Svensson (ed.), *Om Proust. Röster om Marcel Proust, hans tid och hans verk*, Enskede: Marcel Proust-sällskapet 1996, pp. 106–117.

Per Stam, *Krapula. Henry Parland och romanprojektet Sönder*, Uppsala: Comparative Literature Department at Uppsala University/Helsinki: Svenska litteratursällskapet i Finland 1998.

Per Stam, "'Det är redan poesi'. Anteckningar om Henry Parlands litterära metod" ("It Already is Poetry": Notes on Henry Parland's Literary Method), *Historiska och litteraturhistoriska studier* (Historical and Literary-Historical Studies) 83, ed. Malin Bredbacka-Grahn and John Strömberg, Helsinki: Svenska litteratursällskapet i Finland 2008, pp. 215–246.

Per Stam, "Ett småleende utan urskiljning. Nya dikter av Henry Parland" (A Faint Smile without Separation: New Poems by Henry Parland), *Lyrikvännen* 1–2: 2009, pp. 28–32.

Per Stam, "Spring in Kaunas. Henry Parland in Lithuania", *Baltic Worlds*, April 2009 (Vol. II:1), pp. 20–21.

Robert Åsbacka, "Att skriva sig fri. Om Henry Parland och Marcel Proust", *Finsk Tidskrift. Kultur, ekonomi, politik* 1996, pp. 133–145.

2. By Henry Parland

Henry Parland, *Idealrealisation* (*Ideals Clearance*), Helsinki: Söderströms 1929.

Henry Parland, *Återsken* (Reflections), Helsinki: Söderströms 1932.

Henry Parland, *Hamlet sade det vackrare. Samlade dikter* (Hamlet Said It More Beautifully. Collected poems), ed. Oscar Parland, Helsinki: Söderströms 1964.

Henry Parland, *Den stora Dagenefter. Samlad prosa 1* (The Great Morning-After: Collected Prose I), ed. Oscar Parland, Helsinki: Söderströms 1966.

Henry Parland, *Säginteannat. Samlad prosa 2* (Say-Nothing-Else: Collected Prose II.), ed. Oscar Parland, Helsinki: Söderströms 1971.

Henry Parland, *Sönder (Om framkallning av Veloxpapper)*, Pilotserien, Stockholm: Författarförlaget 1987.

Henry Parland, *Sönder (om framkallning av Veloxpapper)*,

edited and with comments by by Per Stam, Helsinki: Svenska litteratursällskapet i Finland/Stockholm: Atlantis 2005.

3. Translations

Henry Parland, *Hamlet sanoi sen kauniimmin: kootut runot*, transl. Brita Polttila, Porvoo, Helsinki, Juva: WSOY, 1981.
Henry Parland, (z.B. schreiben wie gerade jetzt). *Gedichte* (selection of poems), transl. Wolfgang Butt, Sammlung Trajekt 17, Stuttgart: Klett-Cotta / Helsinki: Otava 1984.
Henry Parland, *Rikki (velox-paperille vedostamisesta)* (Sönder), transl. Hannu Nieminen, Helsinki: Tamara Press 1996.
Henry Parland, *Pavasaris kaune* (Vår i Kaunas/Spring in Kaunas; poems, essays, etc.), transl. Petras Palilionis, Kaunas: Ryto varpas 2004.
Henry Parland, *Déconstructions*, transl. Elena Balzamo, Paris: Belfond 2006 (with the novel came a booklet with *Idealrealisation* in its entirety, under the title *Grimaces: Poèmes*).
Henry Parland, *Zerbrochen (Über das Entwickeln von Veloxpapier)*, transl. Renate Bleibtreu, Berlin: Friedenauer Presse 2007.
Henry Parland, *Vdrebezgi. Roman* (Sönder), transl. Olga Mäeots, Moscow: Tekst 2007 (the volume also contains "Stichotvorenija" (Poems)).
Henry Parland, *Ideals Clearance*, Brooklyn: Ugly Duckling Presse 2007.
Henry Parland, *Sudužo (apie "Velox" fotopopierianus ryškinimą)*. Romanas, translated by Agnė Kudirkaitė Ydrauw, Vilnius: Apostrofa 2011.

VICTORIA BENEDICTSSON

Money

(translated by Sarah Death)

Victoria Benedictsson published Money, her first novel, in 1885. Set in rural southern Sweden where the author lived, it follows the fortunes of Selma Berg, a girl whose fate has much in common with that of Madame Bovary and Ibsen's Nora. The gifted young Selma is forced to give up her dreams of going to art school when her uncle persuades her to marry, at the age of sixteen, a rich older squire. Profoundly shocked by her wedding night and by the mercenary nature of the marriage transaction, she finds herself trapped in a life of idle luxury. She finds solace in her friendship with her cousin and old sparring partner Richard; but as their mutual regard threatens to blossom into passion, she draws back from committing adultery and from the force of her own sexuality. The naturalism and implicit feminism of Money place it firmly within the radical literary movement of the 1880s known as Scandinavia's Modern Breakthrough. Benedictsson became briefly a member of that movement, but her difficult personal life and her struggles to achieve success as a writer led to her suicide only three years later.

ISBN 9781870041850
UK £9.95
(Paperback, 200 pages)

SELMA LAGERLÖF

Lord Arne's Silver
(translated by Sarah Death)
ISBN 9781870041904
UK £9.95
(Paperback)

The Phantom Carriage
(translated by Peter Graves)
ISBN 9781870041911
UK £11.95
(Paperback)

The Löwensköld Ring
(translated by Linda Schenk)
ISBN 9781870041928
UK £9.95
(Paperback)

Selma Lagerlöf (1858-1940) quickly established herself as a major author of novels and short stories, and her work has been translated into close to 50 languages. Most of the translations into English were made soon after the publication of the original Swedish texts and have long been out of date. 'Lagerlöf in English' provides English-language readers with high-quality new translations of a selection of the Nobel Laureate's most important texts.

Coming up in June 2011

Lightning Source UK Ltd.
Milton Keynes UK
UKOW021845301111

182979UK00003B/1/P